JOHN BIGUENET

The Torturer's Apprentice

stories

THE ECCO PRESS
An Imprint of HarperCollins*Publishers*

No similarity is intended between the characters and situations depicted in these stories and any persons, living or dead.

Stories in this collection, occasionally in somewhat different form, were originally published in the following: *Denver Quarterly:* "Gregory's Fate"; *Esquire:* "Rose"; *Granta:* "The Vulgar Soul" and "And Never Come Up"; *The Southern Review:* "Lunch with My Daughter"; *Story:* "My Slave"; *Witness:* "The Torturer's Apprentice" and "A Battlefield in Moonlight." "And Never Come Up" was also presented in *Selected Shorts.* "The Vulgar Soul" was reprinted in *The Sun;* "Rose" and "A Battlefield in Moonlight" were reprinted in *The Double Dealer Redux.* Some of the above stories were cited in *The Pushcart Prizes, The Best American Short Stories 1997, The Best American Short Stories 1998,* and *The Best American Short Stories 1999.* "Rose" was reprinted in *Prize Stories 2000: The O. Henry Awards.*

FIRST EDITION

Designed by Cassandra J. Pappas

Printed on acid-free paper

Library of Congress Cataloging-in-Publication Data
Biguenet, John.
The torturer's apprentice : stories / John Biguenet.—1st ed.
p. cm.
ISBN 0-06-019835-4
I. Title.
PS3552.I424 T67 2001 00-055145
813'.54—dc21

01 02 03 04 10 9 8 7 6 5 4 3 2 1
QW

for sha

With thanks to

Jennifer Hengen and Daniel Halpern

Contents

The Torturer's Apprentice

The Vulgar Soul

IT BEGAN AS a chafing, a patch of dry skin, in the palm of his left hand. He ignored it at first, though at odd moments he found himself absentmindedly rubbing the chapped flesh.

It persisted. After a week or so, he appealed to the pharmacist in the old-fashioned drugstore and soda fountain near his house. The druggist, a young man whose diploma on the wall behind him was as fresh and white as the medical frock he donned before counseling customers about their minor complaints, asked the man to extend the hand with the rash.

"It's not a rash, exactly," he said, opening his palm over the counter. "It's just sort of scaly."

"Well, Mr. Hogue—"

"Tom," the man interrupted.

"Well, Tom, I think we've got what you need." The pharmacist led him down an aisle of ointments. Reaching for a purple box, the druggist explained that a simple moisturizing lotion would probably suffice. "But," the young man added gravely, "if itching develops, we may have to consider a hydrocortisone cream."

Sitting in his car in front of the drugstore, Hogue unscrewed the top of the bottle and coaxed a dab of the lotion onto his hand. Massaging the raw flesh with the moisturizer, he saw deeper cracks in the skin than he had noticed before. He poured more lotion into his cupped palm.

That night, peeling off his socks as he dressed for bed, he thought his right foot seemed blistered. *Damn new shoes,* he told himself, though a sly doubt vaguely tormented him as he rubbed moisturizing lotion into his hand. He restrained himself from looking more closely at the blister.

Work preoccupied Hogue for the next few days. The lotion seemed to soothe his chafed hand. The blister, which had engorged itself, burst, and filled again, required some attention, though. He bandaged his foot to prevent infection and waited for his body to heal its own wounds. He smiled at his overblown worries and let them drift away down the broad boulevards of a busy life.

It was with the startled panic of one who suddenly remembers a forgotten obligation that he felt the dampness on the bottom of his sock when he had unlaced his shoe a few evenings later. Slipping the sock off his foot, he was shocked to see the bandage soaked with blood. He hopped into the bathroom and sat on the edge of the tub with his ankle resting on the other leg. Holding his breath, he gingerly peeled back the tape of the dressing. As the bandage came loose, he glanced at the sore and quickly looked away. Taking another breath, he bathed it in peroxide. He was surprised that he could find beneath the cotton ball with which he wiped the blood no open wound, only a deeply chapped bruise the size of a quarter.

By the time Hogue fell asleep hours later, he had convinced himself that there was really nothing all that strange in what had happened. Rushing from meeting to meeting that day, he had done more walking than usual, which must have opened the blister. Tomorrow was Saturday. He would try to keep off his feet over the weekend and give the sore a chance to heal.

Despite two days on the couch with a pillow beneath his foot, by Monday he was hobbled by a tenderness on the bottom of both feet. The blistering had spread to the other foot.

He was embarrassed by the expressions of concern offered by his colleagues as he limped to his office. Though he wore bandages, his gait was deformed by the ache of the two raw bruises on his feet. He tried to stay at his desk all day.

Driving home, he passed the drugstore but thought better of conferring with the young pharmacist when he imagined how ridiculous he would look, tottering on one leg as he laid a bare foot upon the counter. And what if it started to bleed? He often ran into his neighbors at the little store.

Hogue decided to wait. Except for the soreness, he was perfectly healthy. He felt sure nothing was wrong, or so he told himself.

The tenderness eased over the next few days, although there were a few incidents of bleeding. He began to use the moisturizing lotion on his feet. Religiously, he continued to apply the lotion to his hand, but while the dry skin did not worsen, neither did it improve. In fact, it was while rubbing his palms together with a dollop of lotion that he first felt the roughness on his right hand.

He was surprised to find himself almost resigned to his discovery, as if he had been waiting, unknowingly, for this last extremity to exhibit the chafing of the other three.

But there was nothing foreseen in the revelation he received as he undressed one night. Naked before a mirror, he saw a pink circle glowering at him just below his ribs. He watched in the mirror as his fingers inched over his body toward the chapped skin. His hand recoiled as it brushed the intensely painful spot. Suddenly blood began to ooze from it. Hogue lifted his hands to his face; each expressed, drop by drop, thin streams of blood. He did not have to look down to know that his feet were bleeding, too.

It seemed a contradiction to him even as he felt it, but a horror somehow calm and deliberate took hold of him. He held out his hands and watched himself in the mirror quietly bleeding. The terror that rose in him had matured so slowly over the last few weeks, had teased him so often with its acrid taste, that he felt no panic. But he did feel absolutely lost.

THE NEXT MORNING, Hogue convinced the nurse who answered the phone to schedule an immediate appointment with his doctor. He would have to hurry right over, she told him, to meet with the doctor before the regular appointments began at ten o'clock.

He bandaged himself as well as he was able and made himself drink a glass of orange juice.

The doctor was in a jolly mood when he entered the examining room. Hogue tried to think how to begin.

"Something's happening to my body," he said haltingly.

"Tell me about it," Dr. Loewy nodded, dragging a stool closer to the examining table on which Hogue sat.

The doctor didn't interrupt until near the end of the story. "And all five irritations began to bleed simultaneously last night?" he asked with a tone of surprise that worried Hogue.

"Simultaneously," he assured the doctor, "and for no reason."

"Show me," Dr. Loewy instructed.

Hogue removed his shirt as well as his shoes and socks. He let the doctor loosen the five bandages.

Switching on a flexible lamp, the old man examined each area carefully. "I suppose you've tried some kind of lotion? Yes, you told me you did, didn't you?"

Finally pushing aside the neck of the lamp with his arm, the doctor looked up at Hogue. "It looks like some kind of eczema. But just to be safe, perhaps we should get a dermatologist's opinion."

"And the bleeding would be consistent with eczema?"

"It would be unusual," the doctor admitted. "That's why I think we should call in a specialist."

"It couldn't be something more serious, could it?" Hogue asked.

The doctor sighed. "It can always be something more serious. Maybe we'll do a little blood work on you, see what the numbers say." He buzzed for his nurse. "Let Maggie draw a few samples, and then give me a call Friday afternoon around four. I'll let you know what we turn up."

As he opened the door to leave, he added, "By the way, don't bandage them unless they start bleeding again. Maggie will give you the name and number of a dermatologist I work with. I'll give him a call this morning and get him to see you this week, OK?"

Neither the dermatologist nor the lab results shed light on his condition. Everything was "within normal ranges," Dr. Loewy assured him when they spoke on Friday, but he asked Hogue to set up another visit for the next week. "I want to do a little research over the weekend," the doctor said enigmatically.

When he arrived for his appointment on Tuesday, the nurse ushered him into Dr. Loewy's private office rather than an examining room. "The doctor will be right with you," she said.

The desk was crowded with sprawling stacks of files and paraphernalia from drug companies—pads of paper, a pen set, a calendar, a ruler—all of which had been emblazoned with the corporate logos of pharmaceutical manufacturers. A snapshot of a young woman with a child was slipped into a plastic frame imprinted with the name of a well-known decongestant. On the wall was a Norman Rockwell print of a doctor examining a freckled boy.

"I'm glad you're here," the doctor said as he swung open the door, startling his patient. "I've been looking into your case."

It worried Hogue to hear his eczema described as a "case."

"I've found some articles on a condition very similar to yours, something called psychogenic purpura." He held out a copy of *Archives of Internal Medicine.*

Hogue took the magazine but did not open it. "Psychogenic what?"

"Purpura. They're spontaneous lesions—without any apparent physical cause."

"Just like mine."

"Except that your case history doesn't quite fit." Dr. Loewy paused. "There is some other literature, though, that comes a little closer. A blood man I know lent me this." He handed Hogue another publication, *Seminars in Haematology*. "It's got a review of historical cases of your condition."

"So, what is my condition?"

"Have you ever heard of Therese Neumann?" the old man asked as he searched through the files on his desk.

"No, I don't think so."

"On Good Friday in 1926, Miss Neumann, a woman about your age from the village of . . ." Dr. Loewy was distracted as he searched his cluttered desk for a particular piece of paper. "Yes," he said to himself, finding the sheet beneath some folders, "Konnersreuth in Bavaria." The doctor continued to glance at the page, looking for something. "This woman suddenly began to bleed spontaneously from her side. At the same time, her left hand began to bleed from a spot that had been red for days. By nightfall, both hands and feet as well as the wound in her side were bleeding." He put down the paper and looked up. "You're luckier than she was, though. She also had drops of blood weeping from her eyes."

"From the eyes?" Hogue repeated, unsettled.

"Yes, but these eruptions occurred in the midst of an ecstatic vision."

"What kind of vision?"

"Of Christ's passion, of course." The doctor looked at him as if he were missing the point. "My boy, she was a stigmatic—like you."

Hogue wanted to pretend the thought hadn't occurred to him. "Why, that's ridiculous," he objected. "We're not living in the Middle Ages."

Dr. Loewy was searching for another piece of paper. "Yes, here it is. I don't suppose you've heard of Padre Pio? Or the Stigmatic of Hamburg—an interesting case: the man was a Protestant. Very unusual."

Hogue was shocked. "You're a doctor, for Christ's sake. How can you take such superstitions seriously?"

"Superstitions?" Dr. Loewy put down the paper he was holding. "Stigmata are as real as those bloody bandages on your hands."

Hogue looked down and saw the blood soaking through the gauze.

"I thought I told you not to use bandages," the doctor scolded.

"The wounds started bleeding again during the night." Hogue saw the red proof spreading across his palms.

The doctor leaned back in his chair. "Look, I'm a Jew. You think I believe that Jesus is pricking your body to make you bleed? But that doesn't mean you're not a stigmatic. The one in Hamburg, the Protestant, held only the vaguest religious beliefs. But he even carried the wounds of the crown of thorns as well as a bleeding cross on his forehead. He begged his doctors to find a cure."

Hogue allowed himself a smile. "What did the Catholics make of him?"

"He was quite a problem for them. You know, in all the literature, they take real pride in claiming the stigmatics as their own. One of their theologians quickly classified him among the—oh, what was the term?" The doctor shuffled through his papers. "Here it is: the *âmes vulgaires*. The vulgar souls. It was decided that he was 'spiritually mediocre' and suffered from 'psychological blemishes.' What a discreet expression, 'psychological blemishes'! They wrote him off as a hysteric."

"I wonder what they would have said if he had been Jewish?"

The doctor laughed. "Now there's a thorny theological question."

Hogue relaxed a bit. "All right, let's say I'm a stigmatic. What do we do?"

"Well," Dr. Loewy said, growing serious again, "the symptoms are physical. You know, come to think of it, that's the medical term for the characteristic signs of a disease—the 'stigmata.' Anyway, your stigmata are physical, but the cause is clearly emotional. All the lab work came back negative. The dermatologist didn't really know what to make of it, but his report says the sites don't appear self-inflicted. That leaves us only one explanation. You're suffering from a psychosomatic disorder."

"You mean it's stress?"

The doctor seemed uncomfortable with Hogue's interpretation. "Sure, almost everything that goes wrong with the body has to do with stress one way or another. But this is more complicated than that."

"Because I don't feel particularly stressed when it happens. Last night I was asleep."

"It's not as straightforward as simple cause and effect. The body can be awfully mysterious when it wants to. We're complex machines."

Dr. Loewy gave Hogue the name of two psychiatrists. "Talk to them both. See which one you trust."

A question still troubled him. "Is this going to get worse?"

"Well, the classic stigmatics exhibited two or three other symptoms, but you really don't need to worry about them. We've caught this thing in its early stages."

Hogue persisted. "What are the other symptoms?"

The doctor seemed annoyed. He picked up his notes again. "Insomnia, cessation of digestion, and clairvoyance."

"What is 'cessation of digestion'?"

"You stop eating."

"And then you die?"

"No, not according to the literature. There was a celebrated case in the nineteenth century, a woman from Brooklyn named Mollie Fancher. According to fairly reliable witnesses, from the beginning of April until the end of October in 1866, she ate almost nothing—a piece of banana, two teaspoons of wine—basically nothing at all."

"So what happened to her?"

"She got skinny and became a clairvoyant. And she wasn't even a stigmatic." The doctor gave Hogue a sly look. "Of course, she suffered from multiple personalities, so if one of them were to sneak a snack, Mollie might honestly imagine that she had consumed nothing. Like I said, it's a complicated business, this mysticism."

Instead of going back to work after his visit to the doctor as he had planned, Hogue drove to the park across town. It had been built at the turn of the century by a designer who must have loved small, intricate patterns. Narrow walks scrolled around elaborate plantings of delicate flowers and eddied about the feet of carved stone benches in grottoes shaded by weeping willows. In the center of the little park, a modest fountain spilled its water into a vast, shallow pool.

As he circled the fountain trying to come to grips with what the doctor had confirmed for him, Hogue strained to penetrate the shimmering water down to the mosaic arabesques that lined the floor of the pool. He was startled when a mottled, foot-long fish suddenly shattered the mirrorlike surface of the pond as it burst into the sunlight, devouring a mayfly that had lit upon the water. The pool, momentarily animated, quickly regained its tranquillity; the ripples of the extraordinary event were diluted by the stillness of the water before they could reach the arched concrete lip that curled back over the edge of the pool. "Not a trace," he almost said aloud, but a small boy staring up at him (and watched in turn by a woman frowning nearby) stifled his exclamation.

Hogue turned and followed one of the carefully tended paths that spiraled away from the fountain. Finding a wrought iron bench encircling an oak, he sat and tried not to think. He simply watched people—the young couples furtively embracing in the shadows, the old men arguing over chessboards, the women tending children, the swaggering guards puffing up their chests—and felt for them all the most profound sympathy. He was surprised by what he felt, and he knew the ripples of his compassion, if he could call it that, would fade in the spring air long before they could interrupt the kiss of the boy and the girl closest to him, in a little stand of trees about which the path looped back on itself and turned once again toward the fountain.

He realized what he was doing and grew annoyed at his sentimentality. "I'm playing at being a saint, aren't I?" he asked a sparrow that hopped nervously from the bench to the ground and back again.

HOGUE PUT OFF calling the psychiatrists; he was uncomfortable with the idea. It was not long, however, before he had to admit he needed help.

Though it was true that his appetite had diminished over the weeks of swelling worry about his condition, the insomnia was a more pressing problem. It had asserted itself with greater stubbornness after his visit to Dr. Loewy, but when he looked back he remembered bouts of sleeplessness in even the first few nights of his stigmatizing.

He took the first appointment he could get; one of the two psychiatrists, Dr. Burke, had an opening in three days. Fortunately, her free slot was in the late afternoon. He did not want to miss any more time at the office.

Hogue's work had been suffering. Taunted by inescapable worry, he pushed himself from sleepless nights to drowsy mornings to exhausted afternoons that yielded to yet more wakeful evenings. His supervisor's sympathy was souring into anger, but Hogue, of course, could not bring himself to explain. So by the time he shook hands with Dr. Burke in her simple office, he was desperate for a solution.

The psychiatrist wondered if he would like coffee. As he shook his head, he realized that he had stopped drinking coffee. Worried about work, he hadn't really thought about all the ways in which his life was changing. By the end of the first session, he and Dr. Burke had constructed a list of the alterations, especially the inconsequential ones, that had crept into his habits. That was really all the two of them had done, except that she had asked to see his hands. He removed the gloves he had begun to wear in public. She took his hands in hers and turned them over. "You have beautiful hands," she said, almost clinically.

"Except for my wounds," he corrected her.

"Wounds? Is that what you call them?" she asked with surprise, and she wrote something in her notebook.

He felt better afterward and slept for a few hours that night. The next morning, he called Dr. Burke's office and moved up his appointment to the following day.

The psychiatrist was surprised to see him. "I thought we weren't going to meet again until next week."

Hogue nodded. "But I really felt as if we made some progress last time. And I can't go on like this. I've got to do something about my . . ." He almost said "wounds," but he stopped himself.

Dr. Burke asked Hogue to tell her about the last year. Except for the stigmata, there wasn't much to tell.

"I live a quiet life," he explained with some embarrassment when she asked whether he had dated anyone recently.

"What about religion?"

"Well, I'm Catholic—at least I was raised Catholic—but of course I don't practice."

"Why not?"

To believe in God, he patiently explained to the psychiatrist, one has to be willing to close his eyes to a great deal. "Isn't that what they mean by faith—refusing to accept the obvious, refusing to accept what's always been right there in front of us?"

"But that's exactly what believers say," she countered. "God has always been right there in front of us. We just won't open our eyes."

"Maybe it's not so easy to see what's right in front of our eyes."

The psychiatrist laughed. "That's certainly true, Mr. Hogue. I'd be out of business if that weren't true."

"Not that I blame them," he assured her. "In fact, I sometimes wish I did believe. But I'm not going to lie to myself and pretend. It's childish."

He had believed as a child—quite intensely, as a matter of fact, he admitted. But he had outgrown religion. In college, he explained, he had realized that the wildest myths of primitive peoples weren't any more fantastic than the virgin birth or the resurrection of the dead. "The scales," as he put it, "fell from my eyes."

"But to suddenly lose everything you believe in," Dr. Burke interrupted, "surely that must have affected you very deeply."

He smiled and shrugged. "Not really. It all just stopped mattering."

So he found it impossible to accept his stigmata as proof of the existence of God. "What is a miracle, anyway," he protested, "except something science hasn't gotten around to explaining?" He was willing to waver in his atheism; perhaps he even hoped to be unburdened of his lack of belief. But when he looked into himself, he insisted to the woman, he could discern not the slightest trace of faith, not even a doubt.

"I didn't say that your 'stigmata,' as you call them, prove that God exists," she said, and then hesitated. "I just wonder if, in your case, the stigmata might not be simply an extreme form of self-deception."

Hogue was taken aback. "Self-deception? What am I deceiving myself about?"

"I don't know. That's what we have to find out. But your body is mutilating itself. It's demanding something of you, isn't it?"

Hogue understood. "Yes, of course it is."

"Do you know what it wants?" Dr. Burke asked almost in a whisper.

Hogue shook his head.

As his sessions with the psychiatrist progressed, the stigmata bled less frequently. Hogue was getting more sleep, and though he continued to lose weight, he managed to eat something every day. He felt cautiously hopeful.

He had been visiting Dr. Burke for about a month when a letter arrived from the archdiocese's chancery. A Monsignor McRae informed him that a report from an anonymous member of the laity had suggested that Hogue might carry the marks of Christ's passion on his body. "It is the duty of Holy Mother the Church," the letter noted, "to examine all individuals claiming the stigmata of our Lord and Savior."

Hogue's first impulse was to deny any knowledge of the stigmata to which the monsignor referred. But he realized that was useless. Whoever had written to the archbishop—one of his coworkers, a neighbor, someone at the gas station—would continue to see the gloves on his hands, the sudden red spot staining his white shirt as he jerked his jacket closed over it. Eventually, a skeptical parish priest would be enlisted to serve as a witness. Once confirmed, the news would fill bingo halls and churches across the city. Already a ladies' guild or an altar society were no doubt spreading the gossip about the local stigmatic.

So Hogue called the monsignor and asked to meet with him. The monsignor was happy to honor Hogue's plea for discretion; the church had no wish to fan the emotional flames of "miracle hunters," as the cleric derided them. The two men met at a rectory that had been vacated for the evening by the parish's old pastor. "We sent him to the movies," the monsignor explained.

After some chatting about his background (and expressions of relief that Hogue had been baptized a Catholic), the priest asked, "May I see the manifestations?"

Hogue removed his gloves, unbuttoned his shirt, and removed his shoes and socks. The monsignor gingerly touched the reddened spots. "That's it?"

"They bleed," Hogue told him, "at least sometimes."

"Anything else?" the priest asked, obviously unimpressed.

"No, not really." Hogue decided to stay away from the insomnia and "cessation of digestion." He tried to look guilty. "I have to tell you, Monsignor, I'm not a practicing Catholic." Then, to be safe, he added, "Also, you probably ought to know that I'm seeing a psychiatrist."

The monsignor was relieved. "Good," he said.

"So I hope we can keep this quiet," Hogue continued. "I find it all very embarrassing."

"Of course," the priest agreed. "The church is not interested in promoting spectacles. The faithful are easily led astray."

As he pulled away from the rectory that night, Hogue was very pleased with himself. He had portrayed himself as "spiritually mediocre"; he had confessed to "psychological blemishes." He felt sure he had fended off the humiliation of a publicizing of his condition. He even stopped at a bar and had a beer, though he found it impossible to drink more than a few sips.

His elation was punctured when he arrived home. Tacked to his door was a petition signed by five of his neighbors. Above their names, they had simply written, "Pray for us."

Slumped in a chair, the sheet of paper dangling from one hand, Hogue felt desolate. He understood that he could not escape. In a few days, hundreds, perhaps thousands, would know of his wounds. He lowered his head in despair and saw a trickle of blood running down the petition.

The next morning, he peeked out through his drapes to see if the long, sleepless night had finally yielded to dawn. Waiting patiently in the street, ten or fifteen people jostled one another in reverent awe, apparently to catch a glimpse as he walked from the house. "So this is how it begins," he said aloud in the still-dark room.

THAT EVENING he was visited by a representative of the Society of the Paraclete, a group with which he was unfamiliar.

"We are guided by the Holy Spirit to announce the gospel," said the middle-aged man. "Despite the authorities, we believe that we continue to live in the age of miracles. Do you believe in miracles, Mr. Hogue?"

Hogue confessed that he did not.

"Then how do you explain your stigmata?"

He knew there was no point in denying their existence. "I'm seeing a psychiatrist. We're working on exactly what's happening to my body. It's got something to do with stress."

"Perhaps you're right. We certainly wouldn't presume to tell you you're wrong. But have you considered the alternative?"

"I've rejected the alternative."

The middle-aged man leaned forward. "Mr. Hogue, you are involved in something extraordinary. You can certainly choose not to participate in the miracle yourself. But do you have the right to deny others an encounter with the miraculous?"

"It's not a miracle."

"Why not let others be the judge of that?"

The calm, indefatigable representative wore down Hogue's resolve. In the end, an agreement was reached for a single meeting with the group.

Albert Rapallo, the man with whom Hogue had spoken, picked him up the following Sunday night. "I'm sorry for the secrecy," Rapallo apologized, "but the church authorities are rather hostile to our work. We like to joke we're a little bit like the early Christians, hiding from our persecutors. Except our catacombs are just the basements of our houses."

The group of mostly older Catholics greeted Hogue warmly. He declined the coffee that was offered and followed his host into the den. The men, women, and a few children joined hands and offered a prayer that Hogue didn't recognize. Then there were readings from scripture. Finally, the man who had led the service so far asked everyone to sit. "Our good friend Bert is going to introduce our guest," he announced.

Rapallo offered a few words of introduction and then surprised Hogue when he turned the floor over to the bewildered young man.

Hogue didn't know what to say. So he simply peeled off his gloves and held up his hands. He hadn't realized it, but they were bleeding.

"Please," said a woman sitting near him, "may we see the others." She asked so gently and so humbly, Hogue felt he could not refuse. Removing his shoes and socks and lifting his shirt to untape the bandage he always wore now as a precaution whenever he went out, he leaned back in the chair to expose the wounds. The group dropped to their knees and began the rosary.

As they mumbled through the Our Fathers and Hail Marys of their beads, Hogue at first felt utterly ridiculous propped up for their edification in the paneled playroom. But the intensity of their faces, the joy and awe of this moment for them, confirming their most profound desires, swayed his feelings. By the time the final prayers were recited, he felt a great sympathy for these desperate believers. He remembered the afternoon in the park but understood immediately the difference. Then he had been deluded by a kind of ambition; now, though moved by the group's innocent passion, he felt no pretense of sanctity. He did feel, however, as if he had finally resolved something within himself.

Over the next few weeks, he agreed to visit other groups. Invariably meeting in secret, small bands of the laity prayed as he revealed his wounds. They rarely bled, but that did not seem to make a difference. More and more often, the faithful would whisper special intentions for which they asked his intercession. Though he, of course, promised nothing, he did not refuse the woman who prayed for the remission of her husband's cancer, the man who begged for the safe return of his runaway daughter, the couple who wanted a child.

⚓

ABOUT TWO MONTHS LATER, Dr. Burke was awakened by a phone call just after midnight. It was Hogue.

"Did I wake you? I'm sorry. I lose track of the time at night."

She was still half asleep. "Mr. Hogue, no, I'm glad you called. I've been leaving messages for you on your machine. I'd given up on you."

"I'm sorry. It's been so hectic."

"How have you been? Are you still troubled by the . . . emissions?"

She heard him laugh. "Do you mean are my wounds still bleeding? Yes, every so often."

"So, how are you?"

"Well, I'm afraid my secret was found out. The archbishop ruled that I was not a true stigmatic, but the people, at least the older ones, were not convinced. They insist my wounds are a miracle."

The psychiatrist sounded worried. "Is that what you've come to believe?"

Hogue laughed again. "Oh, no. Not at all. I'm afraid my views on religion have not changed in the least."

"How is your physical condition?"

He took a deep breath. "Stable. I try to eat something every day. Not much, but something."

"And sleep?"

"I don't know, I'm so drowsy most of the time. Perhaps I do fall asleep for a few minutes here, half an hour there. That's the worst part really, the insomnia, but at least there's no pain. I've been reading a great deal about stigmata; often there's excruciating pain."

"What about work?"

"I had to give up my job. It got to be impossible, particularly once the premonitions began. They are so distracting." He knew she was writing down the word "premonitions."

"Then how are you managing?"

"I've become a kind of religious celebrity. I display my wounds at someone's house, sometimes an elderly priest will invite me to a secret meeting in the parish hall. That's really all there is to it. And after all, how does it hurt to encourage their belief—even if I don't share it—and to comfort them? They are so tender and innocent in their devotion, like children. You should see them."

"You don't think it's dishonest?"

"How? I don't make any claims for myself. I let them judge with their own eyes. They believe what they want to believe."

There was a pause, then Dr. Burke asked, "And what do you receive in return?"

"They make donations," he admitted. "Not much, but enough for rent. Since I stopped working and sold the car—I didn't think it was safe to keep driving—I really don't spend very much anymore. And of course, they pay my travel expenses."

"Travel expenses?"

"I've been visiting groups in other cities." He chuckled. "They joke that it's a reverse pilgrimage."

"And do they come to your house, these people?"

"Yes, but not as many as you would expect. They're pretty good about respecting my privacy. Of course, I'm getting more and more mail, people asking for favors."

The psychiatrist sounded exasperated. "Mr. Hogue, you have to stop this. It's going to get out of hand."

"Doctor, do you remember when you told me that my body was mutilating itself, that it was demanding something of me?"

"Yes," she said softly.

"Well, I've simply yielded to my body's demands. I don't understand what my body wants, but I do know what will satisfy it. And that's what I'm doing."

"But what about the people you are deceiving?"

"My stigmata are real," he insisted, losing patience. "And I simply don't believe that the cause makes any difference." He took a deep breath. "Listen, if my wounds soothe a dying old man or comfort his widow, if a few drops of my blood help a mother and father over the loss of their baby, should I deny them that consolation?"

There was silence. Finally, Hogue said, "I had a special reason for calling you tonight, Dr. Burke. I suddenly started thinking about you. You're taking a trip somewhere this weekend, aren't you?"

The psychiatrist was surprised. "Yes, to a conference in New York. How did you know?"

"That's not important," he said wearily. "But you mustn't go."

"Why?" She glanced down at her notepad and saw where she had scribbled "premonitions." "Is it the plane?"

"No, not that. All I know is that you just shouldn't go."

"You don't actually believe that you've become clairvoyant, do you?" She was angry.

"I don't believe anything. I just know that sometimes I'm right about these things, and I wanted to warn you."

The psychiatrist's anger was thickening into fear. "You can't expect me to cancel my trip because you've had a vision. It's out of the question."

"You're probably right," Hogue said, trying to calm her. "I just felt I shouldn't decide for you. I thought I owed it to you to call. Please, forget I said anything. I'm sorry." He hung up.

WHEN DR. BURKE knocked at Hogue's door a month or so later, she was greeted by an old woman who demanded to know whether she had an appointment.

"Please," the psychiatrist insisted, "just tell Mr. Hogue that I am here."

A few moments later, Hogue himself ushered the doctor into his study. "You must forgive Margaret," he whispered in a weak voice. "She can be very abrupt, I know. But she's just trying to protect me. They come at all hours now."

The psychiatrist was shocked at Hogue's condition. He had lost a great deal of weight since the last time she had seen him. He was having trouble walking, and his face had grown so pale and sunken that his dark eyes seemed huge. He crumpled into an armchair and flicked off the lamp next to him. "The light, you know," he explained, touching one of his eyes.

"I'm glad to see you," he went on. "I wanted to call to apologize for—"

She stopped him. "You were right."

He winced as if he had been struck. "What happened?"

"I'm pregnant."

Hogue smiled. "That's wonderful. I was afraid—"

"It's not wonderful. It was stupid what happened. What I did."

"On your trip?"

She nodded, then took a deep breath. "I got the test results from the lab this morning." She slid her chair closer to Hogue's. "I've got to decide what to do about this right away."

"Why? You have time."

"I'm married. This isn't my husband's child. He's going to find out." She started to cry. "I love him."

There was a knock, and the door opened. "I brought some tea for your guest, Thomas."

Wiping her tears, the psychiatrist thanked the old woman.

Margaret scowled at her. "He needs his rest."

"I'm almost done," the doctor promised.

Hogue gestured feebly for his housekeeper to leave.

Dr. Burke waited for the door to close. "What am I going to do? Have this child and pretend it's Ted's? Live a lie for the rest of my life? Or should I have an abortion? Or tell Ted the truth?"

"But you don't expect me to tell you what to do?"

The woman took another breath. "I want you to tell me what you saw the night you called."

"I didn't see anything. It was a feeling." He tried to adjust himself in his chair. "I was thinking of you traveling—I don't know why. And I knew you shouldn't go. That's all."

She started crying again.

"I'm sorry." He took her hands in his. "Dr. Burke . . . Evelyn," he said, "don't let me confuse you. You know that what's happening to me is no miracle. It's like you said: my body is simply demanding something of me. And now your body is demanding something of you. That's all there is to it."

She looked into his exhausted eyes and smiled. "They take you for a saint. Maybe they'll take me for a virgin mother."

He laughed weakly.

As she rose to leave, he whispered, "They're wrong, you know. They've always been wrong. It's not the soul; it's the body."

She wanted to ask him what he meant, but the old woman was already at her arm, pulling her toward the door.

⚡

IT WAS some months later, in the heart of the winter, that Margaret first remarked on his appetite. "Thomas, you finished your whole meal. Thank God you're finally eating."

Hogue looked down at his plate. He was shocked to find that he had eaten everything.

That night, he awoke with a start, frightened and disoriented. He put his face close to the red numerals of the clock beside his bed: 4:12, it read. He tried to clear his mind. Had he really been asleep for five hours?

Hogue lay there in the dark, troubled and hungry. He had sensed changes in himself, he had to admit, small things, but changes nonetheless. The blood, when it finally came, was a mere trickle lately, each drop squeezed with enormous effort, it seemed, from the wound. He hadn't paid much attention to it—the bleeding was always irregular. But now that he thought of it, when was the last time he had bled at all?

Over the next few months, he began to gain back lost weight. More and more often, he slept through the night. And the bleeding diminished even further until, by summer, he could find no trace of his stigmata.

At first he had tried to conceal the changes. But as obvious to those around him as had been the onset of his condition, so also was its remission. He increasingly sensed that those who, just weeks before, had crowded round to beg his intercession now regarded him as a charlatan, the agent of a counterfeit miracle. By the end of the summer, Hogue had lost his following. Even Margaret, though sympathetic, parted company with him that September, moving to Seattle to care for an ailing sister.

Like any invalid unexpectedly cured of his malady, he felt—with no little resentment—his sudden abandonment by those who had ministered to his every need. Yet he told himself he was glad to be rid of them all.

Hogue tried to pick up where he had left off. He found a job—nothing like the kind of position he had held before the stigmata, but at least in his field—and he took a cramped but cheap apartment in a different neighborhood. Neither at work nor at home, though, could he recover the sense that things were normal.

He imagined himself, especially in dealings with his new colleagues and neighbors, to be living under an assumed identity. He, of course, dared offer no hint of the extraordinary events of his recent life. When pressed, he alluded to a rare illness that he had contracted but survived. And even if he had wanted to reveal the truth, what proof did he have? No matter how insistently the thumb of one hand worried the palm of the other, no seam of skin, no scar corroborated the existence of a healed wound.

When, having finally conceded to himself that he needed help in this readjustment, he called Dr. Burke's office for an appointment, he was told that she was still on maternity leave. He declined a session with her replacement. Instead, he called her at home. She knew the little park where Hogue suggested they meet.

The woman had taken a bench near the fountain—in the sun for the baby, it occurred to him as he approached. "It's good to see you, Dr. Burke."

She looked up from the child, squinting into the late afternoon light. "Mr. Hogue, how are you? You look wonderful."

"Well, I'm eating again. And sleeping."

"Please, sit down. How have you been?"

He sighed. "It's been strange. Like I told you on the phone, the bleeding stopped."

"And the wounds?"

Hogue smiled. "Is that what you call them?"

Dr. Burke laughed.

"Gone," he said, "not a trace left."

"I noticed you weren't wearing gloves."

"Gloves?" He shook his head. "I'd almost forgotten about them."

Ever so slightly, she rocked the baby in its carriage. "So, Mr. Hogue, how are you really?"

"OK, I guess."

"You sound disappointed. Isn't this what you wanted—to be rid of your stigmata?"

Hogue sighed. "At first, when they began to disappear, I thought I was going to get my own life back. But that's not what happened, not exactly." He looked away. "You know, it's like the world you used to live in is gone, obliterated. Now all you've got is this new world, somebody else's world."

"Mr. Hogue, this is the only world there is."

"Yeah, I guess you're right. It's just that, the whole time people were whispering 'miracle, miracle,' I never once pretended at something I didn't feel, didn't believe. And now that it's all over—I know it's crazy—now I feel like I'm living some kind of lie."

The woman shifted the carriage out of a shadow that had crawled across the path. "You know, I've often thought about what you told me the last time I saw you."

"About the baby?"

"No, at the end, just before I left. It's not the soul, you said, it's the body."

He nodded. "What else could it be? I mean, unless you believe in God and all the rest of it, what else have they been talking about? Jesus, Mohammed, Buddha—if there is no soul, then they're talking about the body."

"I didn't really understand what you meant until Teddy was born."

"That's the baby's name?"

"Yes, after my husband."

"So you didn't tell him?"

"Why? Ted would have been hurt. The baby would have grown up without a father. Where is the good in that?"

"And you don't think it's dishonest?"

She gave an exhausted laugh. "Of course it's dishonest. And don't

worry, the guilt never dulls. But I realized that to save myself from
that guilt I would have to sacrifice the two people I loved most of all,
my husband and my child. Why should I be the happy one?"

The woman dangled her hand above the baby, wiggling her fingers
and cooing the child's name.

"You know," she said, turning to Hogue but leaving her hand
lolling over the edge of the carriage, "maybe neither one of us is living
a lie. Maybe we've just stopped deceiving ourselves, and this is what it
feels like."

The baby was growing restless. The woman lifted him and rocked
him in her arms. "He's hungry," she explained. Discreetly adjusting a
little blue blanket over her shoulder, she unbuttoned her blouse and
offered the child her breast.

He could hear the infant's ravenous sucking beneath the cloth.
"But what were we deceiving ourselves about?"

She turned her face to his, even as she continued to suckle the
baby. "Why, everything, Mr. Hogue, absolutely everything."

The woman shifted her position, and the child, jostled, lost the nipple. Squalling, insistent, he furiously jerked a tiny fist free of the blanket, then grasping a fold in his fierce grip, tugged the blue cloth to the
ground. His mother lifted her shoulder, easing her exposed breast
toward the child's face. Finding the teat, but still whimpering, he nuzzled the milk from her body.

Embarrassed, Hogue looked down and saw the hands in his lap,
hands that had expressed, he understood with a certainty approaching
despair, merely blood.

⚓

SO THOMAS HOGUE carried his secret through the streets of the
city, among the aisles of the corner grocery, intent upon his role as an
ordinary man. And thus he continued to live, the quiet tenant in the
next apartment, the business associate whose name one could never
quite remember, until he was recognized at a cafeteria a few years
later by a former member of the Society of the Paraclete.

"You don't know who I am, do you?"

He looked up from his small table, crowded with a plate of prime rib, a little bowl of mashed potatoes, another of peas, a saucer with a corn bread muffin, a glass of iced tea, and the day's newspaper folded to the editorials. A woman stood before him, balancing a red tray heaped with food. She was about his age, maybe a few years older.

"I'm sorry?"

"It is you, isn't it? The bleeder?"

"I really don't know what you're—"

"I saw you at a meeting," she interrupted, "a prayer service. Bert Rapallo brought you." She wedged her tray onto the table and sat down. "Four or five years ago." Her eyes narrowed. "No, four years ago."

Hogue sighed. "Yeah, I remember."

The woman took his admission as an invitation to unload her tray. She spread her little bowls and saucers of food among his, even as he tried to shepherd his dinner toward his side of the table.

"You were something." She shook her head. "I mean really something."

Her hair was cropped—like fur, he thought. And there was something coarse about her that annoyed him.

He tried to make conversation. "Does the group still meet?"

She looked up from her slice of ham. "I don't know. They were friends of Frank, really." She started to lift the fork to her mouth, then paused. "My ex," she explained.

"Oh, you're divorced. I'm sorry."

"Divorced?" she chuckled. "No, that's not allowed. Frank got an annulment."

Hogue nodded.

They ate silently for a few minutes. She would take a bite from one dish, then push it aside, trying another. Suddenly, she smiled at him slyly. "So, how did you do it? That's what I want to know."

"Do it?" he repeated, pretending not to grasp the question. He realized he didn't even know her name.

"The blood. What was the trick?"

Hogue was struck by the way she ate, moving from plate to plate, nibbling, like a bee in a field of flowers. Now she was on to a small bowl of sweet potatoes smothered in marshmallows.

"The trick?" He thought for a moment. "Getting it to stop, that was the trick."

She laughed, taking his answer for a joke.

He slowly sipped his iced tea, regarding her down the long snout of brown glass. She was a worn but handsome woman. "By the way," he said, lowering the drink, "my name is Thomas."

"I'm Karen." She smiled. "You know, you almost saved my marriage."

"Your marriage?"

"Frank, my ex," she explained again, "he eventually dumped me for Christine Aronson—do you remember her, the blonde with the big chest? Probably not. You were just there the one night. Anyway, Frank told me I wasn't committed enough to spiritual perfection and he needed a 'helpmate' who was. Can you believe that crap? That's what he actually said, 'helpmate.' So he dumped me and helped himself to Christine. After the annulment was in the works, of course."

Hogue was growing uncomfortable with the woman. "That's too bad."

"And then," she went on, "right after I hear he's going to marry her once everything is legal, I get diagnosed." She shoved the potatoes aside with her fork. "Ovarian cancer. Advanced." The woman slid a small cup of chocolate pudding in front of her. "It knocked me for a loop."

Hogue didn't know what to say. "I can imagine," he managed.

"Frank was right—about me, I mean. That's why I let him get away with it when we finally went to the canon lawyer. I had never really bought all that religious mumbo jumbo, but Frank liked it, so what the hell, I thought. After a while, though, Frank could tell what I was thinking, and it made him feel small, silly, I guess. We started fighting about it all the time."

He was confused. "But what did I have to do with your marriage?"

"Well, when you came along and I saw it with my own eyes—the wounds looked like they were really bleeding, I saw them—for months and months, till the next summer when Bert told us the truth about you deceiving us, I was a true believer. That whole year, I was Frank's helpmate. And everything was different between us—better."

"I wasn't trying to deceive anybody."

"It wasn't your fault. I mean, how could it last? What do they call it, a fool's paradise? That's where I was living. But it was paradise, at least for a while."

Hogue tried to defend himself. "There was no trick to it. I really was bleeding."

The woman shrugged. "Nobody blames you. We were lying to ourselves. All of us. And to be honest, for Frank and most of them, it didn't make any difference anyway. But for me, once I knew the truth, that I'd been hoodwinked—no offense, Tom—there was no going back. By winter, we'd already signed the annulment papers, Frank and me."

"And that's when you found out about the cancer?"

"A few months later. They pulled out my plumbing, zapped all the cancer in sight."

"So you're OK?"

"I was. But now it's back—in the lymph nodes. I just finished a second round of chemo last month." She poked one of the sliced peaches with her fork. "But it didn't do any good."

He suddenly realized she had been forcing herself to eat.

"You know, when the doctor gave me the bad news a couple of weeks ago, I thought about you. What if there was something else? That's what I kept thinking. What if you weren't a fake? What if your hands really did bleed?" She laughed and tried the sweet potatoes again. "Crazy, huh?"

Hogue looked at the woman. She was still smiling.

Wiping his lips, he inconspicuously slipped his steak knife under the table in a fold of his napkin.

My Slave

I WAS AWARE that the practice was no longer in fashion, that it was even held in contempt by certain elements of our society. For example, we had recently read of a band of protesters, in one of our larger cities, who had rudely badgered dignitaries arriving for some state function. One or two officials—politicians, really—had courted popular support by interceding with the police on behalf of these vocal abolitionists. But the ownership of slaves was still legal.

I want to emphasize that point: it was perfectly legal. In fact, though the economic benefits to the country had declined with the mechanization of agriculture and the automation of factories, slavery was a tradition still honored in the private sphere. In the houses of our better families, at least here in the provinces, one was always met at the door by a slave, served food by a slave, entertained by a slave. And occasionally, one might even hear, wafting down a marble stairwell, the melodious voice of a slave lullabying the children of the wealthy to sleep.

It could not escape notice that they who opposed slavery were those without the means to own slaves. Envy, in this matter as in so many other economic issues, seemed to fire the great engines of liberal virtues and social principles.

At any rate, my success in the sugar market elevated my financial position to the point where, I realized one day, I might purchase one of my own. Such an acquisition, however, was no simple transaction. The importation of slaves having been outlawed by an international covenant some years before, slave owners rarely traded their stock. The great households so depended upon the vital functions delegated to their slaves that a sudden shortage might paralyze a family. Considering the vicissitudes of a slave's life, a master would be foolish to gamble on the longevity of his servants. Therefore, the few slaves available for purchase were defective, usually, in one way or another. Most often, they were maimed beyond productive use. Occasionally, they were so mentally enfeebled as to be indifferent to the lash. And still the prices were exorbitant.

So the prospective slave owner had to exercise a certain ingenuity. I followed up the occasional leads I had been given at social gatherings, but invariably the sale already had been concluded or the slave had died. Disappointed, I began to court individuals whose fortunes were declining. I reasoned that a desperate debtor, cornered by his creditors, might bargain away—well below market value—an irreplaceable asset like a slave to a sympathetic friend with ready cash.

The fluctuations of the economy soon presented me with a drunken offer from a retired military officer, whose acquaintance I had made a few weeks earlier. Surprised by his proposition but aware of his unfortunate circumstances, I haggled down to a price I am embarrassed even now to reveal. To be honest, I was buying, as the expression goes, a pig in a poke; I had never seen this slave of his. But for what I was paying, I could not lose.

Knowing that my friend might reconsider our bargain if he sobered, I insisted on taking possession of the property immediately. I had a cab drive us to my rooms, where I poured him another drink. As he stumbled toward a chair sloshing liquor across my carpet, I slipped into the bedroom and withdrew my money from its hiding place. I counted out the sum we had agreed upon and stuffed it into my pocket. Helping the colonel to his feet, I led him down the stairs and out into the street.

His house was nearby. Even in moonlight, its shabbiness was visible. An unkempt garden lapped over the slippery stone path to his door. He raised the massive knocker and clapped it, again and again, against its worn brass plate until we heard the bolts slide from their buckles on the other side of the door.

A small, plain woman bowed to us as we entered the once-handsome home. In a gruff voice, the colonel ordered her to bring us drinks in the study. As he fumbled with the souvenirs of his military campaigns that were strewn about the room, pathetically attempting to convince me of his former glory, I wrote out on his own letterhead a bill of sale for him to sign. Almost offhandedly, he scrawled his signature across the document.

Just then, the woman returned with two glasses on a tarnished silver tray. He lifted his drink in a toast to me and downed it in a swallow. Then he told the woman—Aurelia—to pack her few clothes; she could keep them, he said. Aurelia did not understand. "I've sold you," he growled, "to this gentleman." Her face betrayed not the subtlest wince of emotion.

When she returned a few moments later with a small bundle under her arm, the old man seemed, suddenly, to grasp what was happening. To my amazement, this career officer, this hero of the island wars, began to weep. He fell to his knees, hugging the woman around her waist and breaking into sobs. Disgusted, I untangled her from his arms, threw the money on the floor, and plucked the bill of sale from his desk. I slammed the door on his pitiful wailing.

In the cab home beside the silent woman, I was so elated by my purchase that I did not realize how unprepared I was for this addition to my household. A slave would mean changes in my life, but having left for dinner that evening without the least thought that I might return some hours later the master of a slave, I had not yet even begun to contemplate the requisite arrangements. For instance, where would she sleep? Where would I put her when I desired privacy? What lavatory would she use? Having concentrated for months on acquiring what I desired, I had failed to consider for even an hour what possessing it might mean.

As I unlocked my door and Aurelia shuffled in behind me, I found myself confronted by a hundred questions yet to be resolved. The slave stood in the parlor, awaiting orders. Too tired to think my problems through, I told her to sleep on the sofa.

I was continually surprised during our first weeks together at how Aurelia managed to avoid me despite the cramped size of my apartment. Though there were only four rooms, I often had to search for her. Sometimes, I would check an empty room, move on to another, then returning to the first room find her there, seated with her hands in her lap. "But, sir, I have been here for an hour," she would insist when I questioned her. She was so quiet, almost stealthy, that I half believed I might have overlooked her in my first search of the room.

So, many of my fears failed to materialize. Aurelia was never underfoot. She made for herself a place to sleep. She squirreled away her belongings out of sight. There was never a trace of her—except for her scent—about the apartment.

Everyone, of course, complained about the smell of slaves. Their odor was acrid and so very humid. In close quarters with them, it could be nearly unendurable. It was their smell, not their status, that was the cause of their segregation in vehicles of public transport and in the waiting rooms of railway stations.

Eventually, though, a master becomes inured to the smell of his own slaves. I do not mean to suggest that, after a few months, I no longer recognized Aurelia's scent; I simply ceased to find it offensive. In fact, it began to seem not so much a smell, now that I think of it, as a presence permeating my home. Everything was tinged by it. Neither sweet nor foul, it lingered for hours after her hand had passed. She creased it into each cloth she folded. She rubbed it into each apple she pared for me. Even the lemon oil she massaged into my mahogany table could not disguise it.

In this way, Aurelia insinuated herself into all of my possessions. My towels, especially, carried her strange flavor. And I fell asleep each night with my face pressed against her troubling essence in the folds of my pillowcase.

I must confess to a certain clumsiness at first in my handling of Aurelia. Inexperienced in the overseeing of slaves, I knew virtually nothing of the complex mechanisms of discipline and punishment that had been developed over the centuries to maintain the equilibrium of a household with slaves. My lawyer acquainted me with the relevant statutes of the slave code; he explained the few legal limitations on my authority over Aurelia. But for the more mundane problems that arose in the course of my dealings with the woman, I turned to colleagues and members of my social set for guidance.

Everyone offered the same advice: be strict to the point of cruelty. A slave expected as much of a master. If I wanted Aurelia's respect, if I wanted to be able to trust her, I must declare in the most unambiguous terms my mastery over her. My friends feared it might already be too late to set the relationship straight. As one of my mother's acquaintances put it, "You should have beaten her the very first night you brought her home." The old woman made a present to me of a crop she had often used on her own slaves. "It's of no use to me now," she explained. "Arthritis, you know."

I hid the elegant little whip in my closet when I returned home. I was embarrassed to display it in front of Aurelia.

A few days later, a friend at my club asked me how my slave had liked her first beating at the hands of her new master. Others at the card table joined in pressing me for details. When I finally admitted that I had not yet whipped her, I was shocked by the vehemence of their response. I had let them down, they insisted. I had let everyone down. What was I thinking, they wanted to know. Didn't I understand my duty to the others?

It had not occurred to me that the mere purchase of a slave might initiate me into a kind of secret society of fellow slave owners. But I could see their point. Unless everyone lived up to the common expectations of masters and slaves, the system itself was placed in jeopardy.

Late that night, I unwrapped the crop in my closet. I called for Aurelia, who, upon seeing the whip I nervously slapped against my palm, calmly unbuttoned the back of her dress and peeled it off her shoulders. Turning her back to me, she grasped in both hands, as high as she was able, the carved bedpost nearest her. Even in the pale bedroom light, I could make out the web of scars that crosshatched her flesh.

I was startled when, as my first blow landed, she cried out in pain. Nothing before had elicited from her the smallest reaction. Her face, perpetually impassive, now trembled with tears. I struck her again. She begged for mercy. Could it really hurt so much? I brought the whip down on her a third time. She screamed in agony. I decided she was pretending, but concerned that my fellow tenants might complain about the noise in the middle of the night, I tossed the crop into the bottom of my closet and asked Aurelia to bring me a drink. Wiping her tears on her sleeve, she rebuttoned her dress and left the room without looking at me.

I must concede that my friends had been quite right. Aurelia's attitude was much improved. Though I thought I detected a slight wince—perhaps I actually had stung her, a bit—she bowed deeply to me as I left for the office the next morning. When I returned for dinner, the house had been thoroughly cleaned. And if she had been unobtrusive in the past, now she achieved complete invisibility.

When I called her to my bath that night to scrub my back, I was embarrassed to find that she was already sitting behind me on the floor next to the sink. I had undressed in front of her without even realizing she was there.

Perhaps my modesty seems disingenuous. I am not ashamed to admit that I employed my slave as a concubine. She was mine to do with as I pleased. I was completely within my rights to have her maimed, to petition the authorities to execute her if I liked. Was this command, to be loved by me, in comparison to these other possibilities, cruel? I hardly think so.

And really, is there a more intimate relation than that of master and slave? Why should it surprise—let alone scandalize—anyone that a slave, who served her master in every other room of the house, would be commanded to minister to his needs in the bedroom as well?

There's another side to this question. Stripped of her rough gown, divested of my robe and jewelry, we embraced each other not as master and slave but as man and woman—equals, really, in a certain sense. I never asked her to compromise her feelings, to play at emotions she did not possess. I never demanded some false display of passion. She was free to feel whatever she felt. And never once did she object.

Well, once she did, but it was over something small. Clinging to the pleasure of the moment, one makes mistakes. My mistake was to amuse myself by dressing Aurelia in my clothes. Obeying, she lifted my silk nightshirt above her head and let it fall, a curtain between me and her nakedness. I reached for my hat on a chair near the bed. Taking it from me, she lowered the hat onto her head; it slopped over her ears like a bucket. My little slave looked like a child masquerading in her father's clothes. I laughed. For the only time that I would ever see real emotion from her, she ripped off the hat and silk gown, her face blazing with hatred. Then, realizing what she had done, Aurelia got up, naked, and grasped a bedpost with both hands, waiting for me to take the whip from my closet.

I felt guilty; it had been my fault. But I had learned enough by now to know that when a slave expected to be beaten, she had to be beaten. I did not worry about my neighbors' complaints; I whipped her until my arm was sore.

It was a few days later that I failed to find a pair of emerald cuff links in my jewelry box. A week after that, I noticed a small antiquity missing from the mantel. That night, after I had sent Aurelia back to her own bed, I extracted my money from its hiding place; some of it had disappeared.

I waited until morning. My slave, of course, denied everything.

She had stolen it all; of that I was certain. No one else had even been in the apartment. But I was faced with a dilemma. If I reported the theft to the police, they might recover my property, but Aurelia's hands would be amputated—the punishment for such a transgression by a slave. Healthy, she was worth more than the goods she had stolen. But without her hands, she was worthless. However, if I did nothing, she would realize that she could continue to steal with impunity.

To make matters worse, the coastal sugarcane had rotted beneath heavy rains that season. My business would survive till the next crop, but I was facing a difficult time. I could not afford the thefts. I began to wonder whether I could afford the thief.

It took only a few days to find a buyer—even at the price I asked. But in that time, both a silver goblet and a set of pearl studs vanished from my apartment. When the gentleman arrived to take Aurelia, I felt a great sense of relief. Without a word to me, the slave once again gathered her clothes and followed a new master away.

In the mood to celebrate, I went into my bedroom to change for dinner. There on my bed lay the cuff links, the statue, the money, the goblet, and the pearl studs.

Rose

"IT MUST HAVE BEEN, I think she said, two years after the kidnapping, when your wife first came by." The voice on the phone sounded young. "What was that, '83, '84?"

"Kidnapping?"

"Yeah, she told me all about it, how it was for the private detective you hired after the police gave up."

"You mean the picture?"

"Right, the age progression."

"You could do it back then?"

"It was a pain in the ass. You had to write your own code. But, yeah, once we had the algorithms for stuff like teeth displacement of the lips, cartilage development in the nose and ears, stuff like that, all you had to do was add fat-to-tissue ratios by age, and you wound up with a fairly decent picture of what the face probably looked like. I mean, after you tried a couple different haircuts and cleaned up the image—the printers were a joke in those days."

"And you kept updating Kevin's . . ." He hesitated as he tried to remember the term. "Kevin's age progression?"

"Every year, like clockwork, on October twentieth. Of course, the new ones, it's no comparison. On-screen, we're 3-D now; the whole head can rotate. And if you've got a tape of the kid talking or singing, there's even a program to age the voice and sync it with the lips. You sort of teach it to talk, and then it can say anything you want, the head."

The voice was waiting for him to say something.

"I mean, we thought it was cool, Mr. Grierson, the way you two didn't lose hope you'd find your boy one day. Even after all these years."

He hung up while the man was still talking. On the kitchen table, the photo album Emily had used to bind the pictures, the age progressions, lay open to one that had the logo and phone number of Crescent CompuGraphics printed along its border. His son looked fifteen, maybe sixteen, in the picture.

He had found the red album the night before, after his wife's funeral. Indulging his grief after the desolate service and the miserly reception of chips and soft drinks at her sister's, he had sunk to his knees before Emily's hope chest at the foot of their bed, fingering the silk negligee bruised brown with age, inhaling the distant scent of gardenias on the bodice of an old evening gown, burying his arms in all the tenderly folded velvet and satin. It was his burrowing hand that discovered the album at the bottom of the trunk.

At first, he did not know who it was, the face growing younger and younger with each page. But soon enough, he began to suspect. And then, on the very last leaf of the red binder, he recognized the combed hair and fragile smile of the little boy who returned his gaze from a school photograph.

As he thought of Emily secretly thumbing through the age

progressions, each year on Kevin's birthday adding a new portrait on top of the one from the year before, he felt the nausea rising in his throat and took a deep breath. It's just another kind of memory, he told himself, defending her.

He, for example, still could not forget the green clock on the kitchen wall that had first reminded him his son should be home from school already. Nor could he forget the pitiless clack of the dead bolt as he had unlocked the door to see if the boy was dawdling down the sidewalk. And he would always remember stepping onto the front porch and catching, just at the periphery of his vision, the first glimpse of the pulsing red light, like a flower bobbing in and out of shadow.

In fact, turning his head in that small moment of uncertainty, he took the light to be just that: a red rose tantalized by the afternoon's late sun but already hatched with the low shadows of the molting elms that lined the street. And he remembered that as he turned toward the flashing light, lifting his eyes over the roses trellised along the fence—the hybrid Blue Girl that would not survive the season, twined among the thick canes and velvet blossoms of the Don Juan— and even as he started down the wooden steps toward the front gate, slowly, deliberately, as if the people running toward the house, shouting his name, had nothing to do with him, he continued to think rose, rose, rose.

I Am Not a Jew

As he descended the narrow staircase into the hotel's tiny lobby, he thought about Ellen reading in bed. She was beginning to look old, tired. They both were.

"*Grüss Gott, Herr Anderson.*"

The young man at the desk, smiling and nodding, took him by surprise. "Ah, good evening." For some reason, he pointed up the stairs and added, "My wife is staying." The clerk cocked his head as if he didn't understand. "In our room . . . while I take a walk," the American tried to explain.

"*Wie bitte?*"

Anderson knew the expression. He had been forced to use it himself over and over again in the little town, where almost no one, it seemed, spoke English. "Sorry," he had apologized to one shopkeeper after another, "what did you say? *Wie bitte?*" Fortunately, his wife's German was much better than his. She had handled most of the

conversation since their arrival that afternoon, even ordering their dinner at the famed restaurant that was the reason for their detour of
nearly a hundred kilometers to Waldheim.

"*Nichts.*" He shook his head, smiling at the boy. "Nothing."

Anderson turned the knob and opened the door. *"Auf Wiedersehen,"* the clerk called.

The boy regarded the man, waiting for a response. "Yes, *Grüss
Gott,*" he replied. Then, because it sounded to his ear so strange a
phrase, he repeated it in English to himself, "Greet God."

Though it was well after ten o'clock, the light had not yet faded in
the lively *Marktplatz,* which the quaint hotels and cafés surrounded,
but the alleys leading from the town square were already darkening.
Restless, he thought about a bowl of ice cream; earlier, in the window
of a crowded shop, he had seen a photograph of *Kartoffeleis,* ice cream
molded to look exactly like a baked potato trimmed with all the top-
pings. And he was tempted by another photo, of what appeared to be
a plate of vermicelli and meatballs in tomato sauce—*Spaghettieis.* But
the constriction of the satin money belt cinched around his waist
reminded him that he had gained too much weight on this trip
already.

A fountain halfway down a long alley caught his eye. Out of habit,
he looked over his shoulder. The square was bustling with families and
flirting teenagers and old couples on benches—no one suspicious. He
laughed at his hesitation. *You're not in the States,* he reminded himself.

The fountain was really quite small when he got close to it. On its
pedestal, a woman in some sort of native costume stood solidly on
two bare feet, pouring water out of a jar she held in her arms. But it
was the rim of the fountain that drew him down onto one knee to
examine its details more closely. A circle of elegant creatures had been
cast in flight, their notched wings and long, severe faces serving as the
lip of the bronze bowl that caught the endless stream of water cascad-
ing from the woman's jar. He could not tell, in the dimming light,
whether they were angels or devils.

BEYOND THE ALLEY, a quiet street twisted into a modern neighborhood. He did not recognize the trees that overhung the neat row of automobiles along one curb. The housing itself looked cheap but well maintained, with tiny garden plots beside each front door. Postwar, of course, he explained to himself.

He wandered on, surprised by the number of lace curtains pulsing with the blue light of television sets. In one undraped window, he caught a glimpse of a bald man watching M*A*S*H. Then he noticed, in the corner of the same window, a gray cat eyeing him.

Having spent so much time with his wife over the last month in the cramped green Renault they had rented in Paris and in a score of tiny hotel rooms across France and Germany, he was relieved to be alone. Savoring the solitude of the summer evening and its fading northern light, he paid little attention as one street yielded to another, until he found himself on the outskirts of the small town. This last street, more of a road, really, wound up a little hill, then veered away from a cemetery that occupied its far slope. Coming over the crown of the hill, dense with trees, Anderson suddenly found himself in the countryside. At the bottom of the hill, more trees obscured the view of what lay beyond. There the darkness had begun to settle among the roots and the trunks. The man checked his watch; it was getting late.

He was about to turn back when he noticed the strange alphabet set into the plaque beside the arched entrance to the graveyard: Hebrew, he realized with a start.

The gate was ajar. In the declining light, a few wrought iron grave markers were visible among the many headstones. Even from the fence, Anderson could see that each framed a portrait of the deceased. Without thinking, he pushed back the iron gate on its rusty hinges and followed the pebbled path from photograph to photograph.

They were the oldest graves, those with the ornate metal markers, the iron fired and hammered into the curlicues and arabesques popular during the last days of the empire. Some, he found, dated back to the nineteenth century. The headstones were newer, from the '20s and '30s.

The porcelain portraits and hand-tinted photographs had faded within the ovals of thick glass in which they had been sealed, but there was light enough to see the bonnets that fringed the faces of dead infants, soldiers' heads jutting from stiff military collars, patriarchs in yarmulkes, sloe-eyed young women. A lost world, he told himself, buried beneath his feet.

He was fascinated. Though night was advancing up the hill from the woods, Anderson hurried on from grave to grave, intoning aloud each name as he bent before the face of the deceased.

"Steh auf, du Judenschwein!"

The angry growl caught him by surprise. He had not heard footsteps sliding up the gravel path behind him. He turned, still crouched before the grave of a Bella Rosenberg, who had died in 1903 at the age of eleven.

A pimply young man, his head shaved, his black boots studded with silver, leaned over Anderson. Behind the leader, three other boys, all dressed in black with shaven heads and heavy boots, were laughing. One had a crude swastika tattooed on his forearm.

Another of them, the fat one, snarled at him, half jokingly, he sensed. Anderson noticed the boy's yellow teeth, bunched haphazardly behind fleshy lips. He had seen the same thing everywhere he went. Why were Europeans so indifferent to the care of their teeth? he wondered. That thought troubled him only for a moment before a hand with its own swastika raised in scars above its clenched knuckles tightened the collar around his throat and lifted him easily to his feet.

He suddenly realized how deep into the cemetery he had wandered.

"Sprechen Sie . . . ," he began, but it was difficult to talk with the hand at his throat. "Do you speak English?" he whispered.

They ignored his question. The leader took a step forward, push-

ing him in the chest, hard. He would have fallen if the scarred hand
had not held him up.

He thought of Ellen, lying in their bed at the Gasthof Zum Alten
Fritz, reading the guidebook to Stuttgart, their next destination.

"Verseuchtes Judenschwein," the young man hissed.

The fear came in waves, shallow at first but each deeper and heavier than the one before. And as each wave broke upon him, the world
constricted, like the hand tightening around his throat, until he was
alive to nothing but the night birds cawing in the woods at the bottom
of the hill, the darkness thickening as if he were sinking in murky
water, the boys circling nervously around him, their boots scrabbling
on the gravel, their chains chafing link against link, their grunted
taunts, the scent of their sweat and of his own urine.

"Schau mal, der Jude pisst in seine Hose," one of the boys laughed,
pointing to the damp stain spreading across the front of Anderson's
pants.

"Scheisse!" cursed the one that had held the man by the shirt as he
loosened his grip and backed away. *"Dreckige Juden."*

"Juden?" At last, Anderson had recognized the word. *"Nein, nicht,"*
he insisted. "No Jew, no Jew," he said, pointing to himself.

One of them made a joke. They all laughed.

He continued to defend himself, now shouting in panicked, non-
grammatical German, *"Ich non Juden. Ich nicht Juden."* The clicking of
the words sounded wrong to him. He fumbled for the verb. *"Ich ist
nicht Juden."* And at last, *"Ich bin nicht Juden."*

With great relief, he realized he had it right, or nearly so, and turning from one snarling face to another, calmly repeated the phrase like
an incantation over and over again: *"Ich bin nicht Juden."* I am not a Jew.
I am not a Jew.

"Ach," said the leader with a kindly smile, *"du bist nicht 'die Juden'?"*

"Nein, mein Herr," he managed gratefully, *"nicht die Juden."*

"Then maybe you're a stinking Arab," the leader continued.

"Nein, nein. Amerikaner. Ich bin ein Amerikaner." And then, realizing

he had been addressed in English, he repeated, more quietly, "I'm American."

The leader turned to his gang. *"Das Schwein ist ein Amerikaner."* Then he added sarcastically in English, "He says he is not the Jews."

The fat one stepped up to him. "Ah, an American. But not a Jew, eh?"

Frightened, he answered in German. *"Sie haben recht. Amerikaner. Nicht Juden."*

They laughed, and the one with the tattoo said, "Well, perhaps you should go back to America, don't you think?" and pushed him down the path. He lost his footing but caught himself as he went down, his hand skittering over the small, sharp stones. Then, suddenly, without thinking, he was running on the loose gravel. He could hear their hoots. One shouted after him, *"Auf Wiedersehen."* Their laughter hung in the air like smoke.

⌇

HE LOOKED BACK as he reached the gate and saw them kicking over tombstones and spraying something in paint across the desecrated graves. He kept running.

Stumbling through darkened neighborhoods, Anderson tried to retrace his route to the square, but he recognized nothing as he hurried on. The houses, with shutters drawn and windows unlit, did not resemble those he had earlier passed. Twice he heard a car approaching, and both times he hid. The hand that had broken his fall in the cemetery was throbbing; the gravel had raked his palm with a dozen raw cuts, crusted with dirt. He began to think he had taken a wrong turn somewhere. Too frightened to turn back, he pushed on. Finally, though uncertain, he followed a long, looping street that reminded him of where he had begun his walk over an hour ago. Then, just as it seemed that he might be going in circles, he recognized, down an alley, the glow of the *Marktplatz.*

As he crossed the emptying square toward the Gasthof Zum Alten Fritz, where Ellen had by now fallen asleep waiting for him, he heard his name.

"Mr. Anderson." It was Ziegler, the owner of the hotel, sitting alone at the table of an outdoor café. He had introduced himself when the couple checked in that afternoon. "Mr. Anderson, will you join me?"

Out of breath, he managed, "Good evening, Herr Ziegler."

"Please," the old man insisted, gesturing toward the empty chair at his table.

Anderson could feel his damp shorts still clinging to his flesh. He dropped his hands in front of his pants. "I really should get back. I told my wife I'd only be gone a little while."

"Just one drink." Ziegler turned to the waitress, who was cleaning another table. *"Ein Altbier und ein Pils, bitte."* Then turning back to his guest, he smiled. "So you've been looking around, *nicht?*"

Anderson saw he could not refuse the old man. "I took a walk," he said as he sat down. Maybe it was a good idea, he told himself, to have a drink before he went back to the room. Beneath the table, his hands were still trembling with the dregs of adrenaline.

"Ja, I walk at night sometimes, too—when the leg doesn't hurt so much."

Anderson noticed the wedding band on Ziegler's bony right hand. Everything was different here, he reminded himself, everything was reversed. He tried to make a little joke. "We're lucky to have wives who let us out at night, you and me."

"No, Margarete died long ago. Very long ago. It's just me."

The American sighed. "I'm sorry."

"No, no, it was very long ago. No matter."

Anderson could think of nothing to say, but Ziegler did not seem to notice the silence as he finished off his beer.

"Here she is." The girl put a mug of dark beer and a glass of light on the table, along with a slip of paper, and took away the empty mug in front of the old man. Ziegler added the receipt to others under the ashtray. "Now you take your choice, Mr. Anderson. The old beer or the pilsener?"

The American reached for the pilsener.

"You don't like black beer, eh?"

"I'm not used to it."

"It's all I drink," the old German told him. He took a sip. *"Sehr gut.* And yours?"

Anderson tried the golden beer in the long, thin glass. "Lovely, very good."

"So what do you think of our little town?"

The American began to lie, but then the story of his humiliation in the Jewish cemetery spilled out of him. "I was all alone," he explained. "There was no one else there, and it was getting dark."

"Das ist schrecklich. Terrible, terrible," the old man nodded, as if he had heard the story before. "They are just hooligans, those boys . . . isn't that your word, 'hooligans'?"

But Anderson was not finished. "I was so frightened I didn't even think. I just started shouting, *'Ich bin nicht Juden. Ich bin nicht Juden.'"*

"Kein Jude," Ziegler corrected, then added gently, "You had no choice. What else could you do?"

The weary American did not try to resist the old German's formula. "Yes, of course, what else could I do?"

"Anyone would have done the same thing. Who could blame you?" The affable owner of the small hotel tried to change the subject. *"Ach,* you know we have a saying: *Wenn einer eine Reise macht, so kann er 'was erzählen."*

Anderson couldn't follow the German. *"Wie bitte?"*

The old man drained the last of his beer. "When one makes a trip . . ." His English was starting to falter. "When one makes a trip . . ." But then he had it. "When one makes a trip, he comes home with stories." Shrugging in sympathy, Ziegler opened his mouth in a smile. His false teeth were white and perfectly straight.

The American emptied his glass. "You are right, Herr Ziegler. What else could I do? Anyone would have done the same thing."

"It's terrible, yes, but who could blame you?"

Now Anderson sounded almost like a man who had been offended. "Yes, who? I'm not a Jew. Is that my fault?"

"Exactly."

The American nodded, returning the old man's smile. Then he called the girl over. "Two black beers, *bitte.* "

Overhead, the vague churring of machinery and the creaking open of iron doors atop the town's ancient bell tower passed unnoticed by the men. Unseen, a bronze axman trundled out onto the ledge of the tower, pausing just before the face of the great clock. Jerking his head ominously toward the now nearly deserted *Marktplatz* forty feet below, the woodsman raised his axe and brought it down, again and again. In daylight, the hour was tolled with each fall of the axe. But darkness had descended, and no bell echoed the twelve blows that fell silently above the sleeping town.

NEITHER THE NEXT MORNING over their breakfast of *Brötchen* and tea, nor during the long drive through Germany and France back to Paris, nor even on the airplane home to Cincinnati did Peter Anderson tell his wife about the incident in the Jewish cemetery. But like a lump beneath the skin one pretends to ignore, the terror of that encounter called attention to itself with greater and greater insistence the more he tried to forget.

Anderson could not glimpse a headline of a new peace accord between Palestinians and Israelis, could not inadvertently tune the radio to an opera in German, could not pass a cemetery at twilight without the copper tang he had first tasted that night in Waldheim leaching up his throat. To his surprise, though, he felt anger not at the skinheads who had bullied him but at Bella Rosenberg, the dead child before whose faded portrait he had been kneeling when they accosted him, and at all the Jews in that little graveyard. He was ashamed, of course, to blame the victims rather than the vandals—and he forced such ignoble sentiments down with the bile that rose from his gut— but if he was honest with himself, he had to admit that it felt to him as if the Jews were at fault, in some sense, at least, for what had happened.

And it was not only for his humiliation in the cemetery that Anderson needed someone to blame: he was slowly discovering he had returned from Europe a different man. When, for example, their first week back, Ellen had suggested after dinner they catch a movie downtown at one of their favorite theaters, her husband told her of the murder behind an office building on Fourth Street he had read about in the *Enquirer;* perhaps they should wait for the weekend and see the film at the mall in Kenwood, he cautioned. Then, picking up some groceries at Kroger's, he annoyed his wife by circling the lot until a spot near the door opened up. "What are we—old people who can't walk a few steps?" she complained. Anderson had no answer for her; he didn't know why he had passed up all the slots in the outlying rows. But the most disturbing change revealed itself in their bed.

Though deeply disappointed when, early in their marriage, they had learned they would never conceive a child, the couple discovered that the freedom from birth control allowed a spontaneous and vital intimacy that often verged on the daring. It was their secret pride, the intensity and imagination of the sex between them. But for the first time, Anderson found himself sometimes impotent in the arms of his wife. She explained it away as simple exhaustion from the long trip they had taken, but he felt it as another pang of the shame to which he had awakened each morning since his night in Waldheim.

That shame was most rawly felt when he recalled the sensation of his underpants dampening. It was ridiculous, he knew, but the warm, wet cloth clinging to his belly, the acrid smell of his own urine, the surreptitious gesture of dropping his hands over the stain, and then back in the room balling up the moist shorts in the bottom of the trash can so Ellen wouldn't find them in the morning—that childish mortification of wetting his pants, more than any other, unnerved him.

As Anderson cowered under its taunts, the memory of his humiliation goaded his increasingly bitter outcry against the Jews. After all, he reasoned, those four ignorant thugs in the cemetery hadn't invented the swastikas tattooed on their bodies. They themselves hadn't fixed on the Jews as the source of their unhappiness. No, he reassured himself, those boys had simply repeated curses thousands of years old. And what was it, after all, about the Jews that had provoked the hatred of their neighbors century after century?

These feelings festered for weeks before he mentioned the incident in Germany offhandedly as he and Ellen drove home from an afternoon of shopping.

"But why didn't you tell me?" his wife asked, dismayed as much by his silence about it as by his story.

ON COUNTLESS OCCASIONS in their marriage, the man had deferred to his wife: to her gift for languages, her sense of direction, her memory of recipes, her insistence on one imperative or another. He knew enough of himself to recognize that his confidence in the woman sometimes withered into intimidation. So Anderson was not entirely surprised when Ellen questioned him over dinner about the events he had recounted on the way home. He had hoped for her sympathy, her unhesitating support. Instead, she probed the circumstances of the incident: why he had taken a walk to the outskirts of town so close to nightfall, what exactly the boys had said, how he had responded.

He was annoyed by her interrogation and resorted to Herr Ziegler's reasoning when she pressed him for further details. "I had no choice. What else could I do?"

"I know, you must have been very frightened."

"No, not frightened," he objected, stung by the word. "But I had to be realistic. We were all alone. It was just me and those Nazis."

He paused, waiting for Ellen to agree.

"Anyway," he continued, irritated by her silence, "what would have been the point?"

Still she didn't answer him.

"Would you rather I'd been beaten?"

"No, of course not," she sighed. "But did they actually say they were going to beat you?"

"Well, what the hell do you think they were going to do with me?"

"I don't know. It's just—"

"You're my wife, for Christ's sake. You ought to be damn glad I got away. They could've killed me."

"I'm just trying to understand what you did."

"What I did? You ought to be worried about what they did, those punks."

"I just never imagined my husband, you—"

"I'm not a Jew. Is that my fault?" he interrupted indignantly. She had been sharp with him since Germany, he felt, even growing testy of late over the waning of their intimacy.

The woman was not finished, but he shied from her scrutiny. "Anyone would have done the same thing," the man insisted vehemently and pushed himself away from the table.

The couple avoided each other the rest of the evening, but as Ellen lay in bed that night watching her husband undress, she returned to his story. "You lied, you know."

"To whom—to you? It's all true, every word of it."

"No, not to me. You lied to those Nazis in the cemetery."

"How was that a lie? I'm not a Jew." He was tired of talking about it and cross with her for bringing it up. *"Ich bin nicht Juden."*

Ellen stared at him over the bed. *"Wir sind alle Juden,"* she whispered.

"Wie bitte?" he sighed with exasperation, playing her little game.

"We are all Jews."

Anderson looked at her uncomprehendingly.

"After Hitler," his wife explained almost tenderly, "what choice do we have? We have to be Jews, all of us."

The man scoffed at her sentimentality. "So what was I supposed to do? There were four of them."

"I don't know," Ellen admitted. "But one way or another, you wound up on the wrong side."

Now he was angry. "You're making this too complicated."

"No, it's really very simple," she continued, stiffening. "In the cemetery that night, they split the world into Jews and Nazis. And you weren't a Jew."

Long after Ellen had fallen asleep, her back to him, Anderson lay awake, rehearsing in his memory those few minutes of terror he had endured on that darkening German hilltop of skulls and bones, refining the little drama with each rendition until his own role was reduced, in the end, to the simple formula that had saved him: "I am not a Jew."

He mouthed the words.

The bedroom's silence, riffled only by the fluttering breaths of his sleeping wife, shamed him.

"So what should I have done?" Anderson appealed to the darkness. But he waited in vain for the solution to offer itself.

Lunch with My Daughter

SHE DOESN'T KNOW I'm her father. In fact, her father doesn't know I'm her father. I mean, the man married to her mother doesn't know. He thinks Frannie is his.

We've all been friends for a long time. Frannie used to call me Uncle Stan. Now she's Francine, and I'm just Stan.

She called yesterday to say she needed to talk to me. I suggested lunch.

So we sit here, silent behind leather-bound menus. She doesn't ask me to translate the French anymore, the way she did three years ago. Now she knows what *canard aux pommes* and *sorbet citron vert* are. She asks what I recommend. Try the *crabes mous*, I tease, and Frannie laughs. The last time we were here, I offered her a bit of my soft-shell crab. Oooh gross, she said.

Her mother doesn't know she called me, and neither does her

father. It's impossible to talk to them anymore, she laments. They don't understand her. I try to curb my sympathy.

She is sixteen. Sixteen. I suppose most men would say, Where has the time gone? But not me; I know where it has gone. Ask any exile. He will tell you where the time has gone.

And it's worse when one is exiled so near to home and happiness. In return for my silence over all these years—and what would have been the point of saying anything once she decided to stay with her husband?—Frannie's mother has slipped me the odd invitation to a ballet recital or birthday party, to a barbecue or graduation. But it's like being a ghost and watching someone else living your life for you. Joe's a nice guy; we're friends, in fact. But he's the one Frannie calls Dad. He's the one who goes upstairs with Meg after the party.

Her parents won't let her go skiing with friends. Yes, she admits, there'll be boys on the trip, but if all she wanted to do was to sleep with someone, she wouldn't have to go all the way to Vermont to do it. I pale a bit. Her parents just don't trust her, she declares.

She pouts just like her mother. I try to be understanding, but I, too, am horrified at the idea of her spending a weekend in the mountains with—the term sticks in my throat—boys. I mention AIDS, but I don't know if I'm trying to protect her or just trying to keep her out of the clutches of those pimply adolescents. She reaches across the table to give me an affectionate, condescending pat on my hand that scares me to death. I remember what I thought of talks like this one when I was a teenager. I try again, telling her about the guy in my building who's dying of AIDS. She grows impatient with me, saying she and her friends know all about it. And they know what to do, she adds ominously.

But this is not what she wants to talk about. It's not why she called me. I prod her a bit, and she says that she doesn't know if she should be talking about it at all, but she had to speak to someone. I nod.

Her parents, she whispers, are getting a divorce. They haven't told her yet, but she overheard them arguing a few nights ago.

I am shocked. I haven't heard anything about this from either one of them. I ask if she is sure.

Her mother told her father he only had to wait another two years—till Frannie was in college—and it would all be over. Then he could run away to Tahiti with his damned secretary for all she cared.

Frannie seems more curious than concerned, but I've learned what deep rivers her feelings can be. Three or four summers ago, we all met for a weekend at the shore. Frannie and I were sitting under an umbrella, reading magazines and laughing at a little kid who was chasing seagulls, when she suddenly turned to me and asked if I had ever wanted to kill myself. That night, worried, I mentioned it to her mother, who explained that one of Frannie's teachers had committed suicide during the Christmas holidays. It's all underground, her mother sighed, it's always been that way with her. All of a sudden, you find out she's been thinking about something for months, but it's the first you hear about it.

That's the way it always was with her mother, too, I remember. It occurs to me that this whole thing about getting a divorce when Frannie goes away to school may be one more example of it, in fact. I can imagine Joe standing there, probably in the kitchen, in the middle of an argument with Meg, when she suddenly explains that, yes, of course they're getting divorced in two years. He asks what in the world she's talking about, and she looks back at him with those huge eyes of hers as if this is something they agreed on long ago—doesn't he remember? No doubt it's the first time he's hearing of it, but that won't make any difference. He's done for.

I'm like that android on television. My head jerks just the slightest bit to the right as if I'm trying to find something in my memory banks, searching for some routine programmed years ago to be activated at an unspecified date in the future when Meg again became a possibility.

So what should she do? Frannie asks, trying to get a piece of lettuce into her mouth.

I stop myself from telling her to cut her food. Instead, I smile reassuringly. People say stuff like that all the time, I promise her. It's nothing to worry about.

She is certain I wouldn't divorce my wife—if I had one.

That's true, I agree, but sometimes love doesn't last.

She nods gravely. Even at sixteen, she already knows I am right about that. Crunching her salad, she wonders if I have ever been in love.

Once, I answer, staring at my plate.

She puts down her fork and demands the details.

I'm noncommittal. It was long ago. It didn't last. Yes, the woman was beautiful, but it didn't last.

Frannie wants to know why. Did she love someone else?

I shrug.

Frannie sees I'm not going to tell her anything about it and, with a little smirk, goes back to her salad.

I was telling the truth. I don't know whether Megan loved her husband back then or not. That last time we were together, when she was sure about the baby, she told me she couldn't bring herself to hurt Joe. I guess that's love—not wanting to hurt somebody—though I told myself at the time it was nothing but pity. At any rate, Meg had her reasons; I just don't know if they had anything to do with Joe or me.

Frannie asks about Paris. I go there once or twice a year on business. She wants to know about my favorite place in the city.

There is a fountain, I tell her, a huge pool really, in the Tuileries Gardens, and every evening about five, all the mothers in the neighborhood take the kids there to wait for their papas coming home from work. The children rent red or blue sailboats from an old man, and the pool fills with a flotilla of little sloops, heeling in the evening breeze. One by one, the fathers arrive in their impeccable suits, copies of *Le Monde* tucked under their arms, and sit beside their wives on the wrought iron benches and green chairs of the dusty park. In half an hour they're all gone, off to their homes for a dinner of onion soup and soft-shell crabs, I say wistfully, and then smile.

Frannie overflows with mock sympathy as she describes the poor

American businessman, sitting alone in the darkening gardens as the old goat-faced vendor gathers up his sailboats.

Goat faced?

She made that up, she concedes, and reminds me about my promise to take her to Paris one day. Then we could sit in the park together at twilight, and I wouldn't be alone.

I haven't forgotten, I assure her.

Maybe if her parents get divorced, we could move there, she suggests, forever.

She's still a little girl, I realize. She makes me agree at least to think about it.

Where will we eat, she wants to know, when we move there? I know better than to permit myself fantasies about a shared life with my daughter. But she wants to pretend, and I have never been able to disappoint her. In a *couscouserie,* I tell her.

I wait for her to ask what that is, and then I explain about Algeria and colonialism and couscous. I promise she will love it.

No, she decides, she will cook for me each night—after we get home from the Tuileries. When I ask what she knows how to cook, she tells me lasagna. And chocolate chip cookies, she adds.

She explains how we will take trips through the countryside. For some reason—a photograph in her French textbook, I guess—she wants to go to Lyon. And Nice, to go swimming, she remembers.

It all sounds lovely and childish, and I smile indulgently as my daughter unfurls her secret plan, until I realize that is pretty much the way I have imagined life with her and her mother all these years. Lasagna and chocolate chip cookies and Nice, to go swimming.

So what do I think? she wonders..

I think I really am that pathetic figure sitting in the darkening gardens with the old goat-faced man. Great, I tell her, I'll look for an apartment the next time I'm in Paris.

She giggles. I'm not like her parents, she says with admiration. Her mother, particularly, refuses to take her seriously. Why can't adults treat kids with respect? she wants to know. Her mother lies around the house all day and fights with her father all night, then turns around and punishes Frannie for the slightest mistake. It's not fair, she complains.

I try to change the subject, but she is not finished with her mother's failings. As the anger bubbles out of her, I am hurt by her devotion to her father and her readiness to take his side against her mother. I, on the other hand, have to suppress one excuse after another for her mother's behavior. It's hard, I want to tell her, to live for twenty years with someone you don't love. But of course, I don't tell her. I nod. I try to temper her feelings. I soothe her. I get her to admit her mother loves her and she loves her mother. As the entrées are served, she tells me that, yeah, she guesses I'm right. She just wants to be taken seriously, that's all.

Frannie loves the shrimp. How's the duck? she wonders, with a sly smile. I dip a large piece in the sauce and let her nibble it from the end of my fork. She blots her lips with the napkin. Good, she says, but not as good as the shrimp.

Something occurs to me. Has she ever tasted duck before? I ask. No, never. This is the first time. But it's good. She likes it.

I try to remember the last time I had something for the first time. I can't think of anything, other than a few chichi vegetables at some dump in the Village a few months ago. But for Frannie, it's all new. It's the Garden at dawn, for her, and everything is waiting for a name.

I want to believe that Meg will have me when she throws Joe out, that Frannie will learn I am her father and throw her arms around me. But I know it won't happen, none of it. Nothing will change.

A waiter trundles the silver dessert cart, overflowing with sweets, past our table. Frannie wants to know if she can have two desserts, one chocolate and one something else. It's an old joke between us, from when she was very small. We're not finished yet, I object. Oh, Stan, my daughter laughs, you eat too slow. She pops the last shrimp into her mouth.

It's the "Stan" that drives the needle through my heart. I can't help

myself. I call the waiter back. The young lady will have one of everything on the cart, I tell him.

Everything? Frannie squeals, delighted. She can't believe it.

I watch her as the cakes and chocolates and strawberries and pies
and parfaits are laid before her. Her eyes, her huge eyes, flash with the
wonder of it all.

A Plague of Toads

IT HAD BEEN easy to discount the tales with which anthropologists entertained us about the superstitions of our Indian countrymen. Beneath the dense canopy of the rain forest, our little brothers with their fanciful names invoked deities that were literally found within each creature—large and small—that padded over the damp and seething soil of the forest floor, that slung from dripping limb to limb in the crowded ceiling of the world, that squawked from perch to rotting perch through the humid air. Bereft of our knowledge, what were these little people to make of sudden death, of famine, of every unexpected tilt of the natural order? Surely one might generously commend their superstitions as at least a tentative, if primitive, cosmology. But who would propose to dignify their lore as a science superior to our own?

Yet after days and days of rain in the city, our befuddled herpetologists yielded to shamans to explain the proliferation of toads that had mysteriously clogged the sewers and storm drains, that had polluted the stairs of public buildings with their insoluble slime, that had hiccuped their way into the recesses of our closets. Having abandoned the theories of modern biology, our newspapers began to carry articles (at first as fillers among the classified advertisements, then as human interest stories in their midweek "Style" sections, and finally advancing—page by page—toward the day's headlines) about historical accounts of downpours of toads.

It was in the midst of this amphibian inundation that I was to achieve my brief notoriety.

Lola and I had been seeing each other since Lent. The afternoon rains of early summer were an excuse for us to prolong our siesta in the cool sheets of my big bed beneath the gentle revolutions of the overhead fan. Occasionally, Lola would tiptoe to the lace curtains that draped the open doors out onto the balcony to see whether the rain had slackened sufficiently to dash back to her job at the tobacconist's a few blocks away. (I would kiss her fingers each time we met, tasting the bitter tang of rosewood and ebony, of greenleave and cherry wood. Were I not so scornful of the scrawny café intellectuals with their swollen pipes and berets, I would have taken up the vile habit, just for the pleasure of the memory-fragrant smoke.) She would stand shimmering in the green light of the stormy afternoon, her dark flesh against the white curtains, modestly covering her nakedness from any poor drenched pedestrian who might be splashing back to work and, as well, from the unemployed machinist in the apartment across the street, who spent his afternoons drinking tea and staring out his window into my room. I encouraged her to check the weather not to rid myself of her company, as she sometimes complained when I became too insistent, but to indulge myself—drowsing in the bed—in the magnificent view concealed from the world by my lace drapes.

So bloomed our idyllic bower of happiness until, toward the end of summer, I received a damp letter stamped with the great seal of the city's mayor. The honor of my presence was requested at a conference of politicians and engineers to confront the growing nuisance of what had begun to be referred to in the popular press as "the plague." I was inclined to ignore the summons: it was true I had won a degree in engineering, with second honors, at the Jesuit university in the old provincial capital and was therefore listed in the national registry; but in the intervening decade, I had never practiced the profession.

This was, of course, in the days before computers and calculators. The iron trestles that spanned ragged gorges and groaned under the weight of infernal locomotives dragging rusting hoppers of ore out of the coalfields of the north, the spider-work suspension bridges that twisted with hyperbolic vibrations beneath hundreds of pairs of feet crossing the wide rivers that sundered our coastal cities, the bent-neck towers that rose to house the natives driven from forests recently "reclaimed" (as the government phrased it)—all these marvelous monuments of faith in the engineer's calculations were shorn up not so much with steel as with ivory. These edifices of modern civilization depended upon not metallurgy but the now extinct technology of slide rules. Alas, I despised the yellowing slabs of elephant tusk upon which finely graduated tables had been scored. Perhaps I resisted the slide rule as the emblem of my father, who had demanded my matriculation in the faculty of engineering rather than in the conservatory of music, as I would have preferred. Nonetheless, once enrolled, I dutifully extracted an education from my professors, winning, as I have said, second honors.

Unhappily for my father but fortuitously for me, the old man died in the arms of his mistress one humid evening a week before my graduation, bestowing on me an inheritance sufficient to preclude the necessity of practicing my detested profession. Too late, I felt, to undertake the study of music, I devoted myself to a career, if that's not too presumptuous a word, of freelance journalism.

It was this avocation that prompted me to accept the mayor's invitation. I was further encouraged, I should add, by Lola's rather enthusiastic endorsement of the conference. Though she had been perfectly happy with me, undistinguished as I was, the notion of marrying (I assure you, it was the first time it had come up) someone from whom the mayor sought counsel in times of civic emergency seemed to thrill her. And if just once you had seen Lola pressing herself against lace curtains as terrifying bursts of lightning illuminated her dark body in my little room, you would have understood my eagerness, in those days, to thrill her.

City Hall, a relic of the colonial administration of the Spaniards, had its majestic steps roped off when I arrived by streetcar for the first session of the conference. "Slime. From the toads," a guard explained, pointing me to a side door. The canes upon which young men leaned in the cloakroom and the mayor's own sleek wheelchair attested to the policeman's warning that one had to watch his step, even on flat ground.

The conference opened with the obligatory exhortations of the assembled engineers by civic leaders, rallying them to find a solution to the vexatious plague (even politicians had by then resorted to the term). I scribbled copious notes as each speaker bombasted the engineers, who sat—neat in their short-sleeved white shirts with the despicable slide rules dangling in leather sheaths from their belts—beneath the stately chandeliers of the great hall. After a luncheon banquet during which the pontifications of City Council members were interrupted by the chirping choruses of toads in the air shafts, the engineers were at last allowed a few hours to discuss solutions to the dire situation outlined by our elected officials.

Not unexpectedly, at least from the point of view of one as jaundiced about the profession of engineering as I, the click of slide rules produced no grander scheme than a proposal to widen the storm drains of the city to accommodate the burden of the present crisis. Of course, as further clicks determined, the project would take at least 11.5 months to complete. And—click, click—require the destruction of every major roadway in town. The engineers, slipping their pens and pencils back into the pocket protectors they wore on their shirts, beamed with pride at their calculations.

"No," interrupted the mayor, raising himself up on the arms of his wheelchair, when the engineers presented their conclusions, "we want you to get rid of the toads. We want them to go away."

The chief engineer, or at least the oldest engineer, seemed genuinely shocked, with the innocent confusion of a theoretician asked after his lecture on advanced ballistics if he wouldn't mind, by the way, shooting a pesky neighbor who was engaged in an affair with the questioner's wife.

"Well, no," he stammered, "I don't know, that is to say, we don't know . . . and, moreover . . . ," and then, unable to finish the sentence, he simply stopped, slipped his slide rule into its case, and hobbled out of the hall on his crutches, mumbling to himself.

Bickering broke out between the engineers and aides to the politicians. The toads, which must have entered the room through the door left open by the exit of the chief engineer, hopped among everyone's feet. As the conference degenerated into a chaos of abuse, I gingerly crossed the broad expanse of slippery pink marble, inlaid with delicate slivers of black and green stone, to an inconspicuous door that I hoped might provide me an exit.

Instead, I found myself in a narrow service corridor, lit by bare lightbulbs, that descended into the vast basement of the building. Faded graffiti boasted of the sexual prowess of, apparently, the wives and daughters of coworkers—violent attempts at erasure were obvious in nearly all cases. However, no one had bothered to efface the vulgar and rather cruel caricatures of the current mayor and his illustrious predecessors that adorned both walls of the passageway. It seemed an ancient tradition, this satiric portrait gallery in the bowels of City Hall, and I descended through centuries of mayoral history, arriving finally at a crude and barely visible charcoal of Suarez y Vallejo, our national hero, who moved the capital from the malaria-infested swamps of the south to the verdant coastal plain that was to become famous throughout the world for its epidemics of yellow fever. Our city's first mayor, crudely depicted in an act of fornication with a sullen-faced Indian, faded on the wall beside an iron grating

that creaked open on rusty hinges. The corridor, interrupted every so
often by locked doors, continued to spiral down into the very earth, it
seemed, so I lifted myself through the small opening that the grate
had secured.

As I lowered myself into a tiny room, not much bigger than a
closet, really, it occurred to me that I'd not encountered a single toad
or heard even one rasping bleat since I had fled, in disgust, from the
grand hall above. It was silent as a tomb.

I found a switch and flicked on a failing bulb, which throbbed with
weak light and cast an amber patina over massive archival records.
Bound in mangy leather, the huge volumes were shelved chronologi-
cally, the flaking golden numerals on their spines representing more
than a century of real estate transfers and property tax levies—or so I
mistakenly guessed. In fact, as I was about to discover, the books con-
stituted an official chronicle of the city that documented the first hundred years of its history. Maintained by Franciscan friars, the chronicle
recounted the efforts of local officials to "baptize and civilize" the
indigenous tribes. The devout authors detailed, incidentally, the daily
life of the capital in its first, perilous century. All this I learned in a few
brief hours as I dislodged one moldering volume after another from
their shelves.

The tantalizing, ambiguous nuggets of history I extracted through
my cursory examination of the chronicles and, especially, the smatter-
ing of references to a "Lost Empire" in the earliest volumes pricked
both my curiosity and my ambition. What a history I could write with
such sources! What fame! What fortune! And most of all, what a shiv-
ering thrill would tickle down the long, sinuous spine of my Lola!

It was as I carefully reshelved the volumes I had plucked at random
that I first discovered the missing year. Puzzled, I started in one corner
and slowly paced around the room, reading the gilded dates in the
wheezing light. There was no doubt about it; a volume, about a third
of the way through the century, was gone. Otherwise, the collection
seemed complete.

Although there was a door out of the room, I decided not to take a chance on getting caught and, flicking off the light, crawled back through the little window that opened onto the corridor, swung the grate back in place, and retraced my steps to the great hall.

Dirty brown light floated above the pink marble floor, which now glistened with slime. Clinging to the wall, I made my way to a door. It was after seven, and the building was nearly deserted. As I carefully shuffled down slick corridors looking for an exit, bellowing heaps of toads twitched in every corner.

When I swung down from the trolley steps, the striped canvas awnings of the shops on my street still bellied with water from a late afternoon deluge. Tadpoles riffled the silver puddles that swelled in the gutters each day with more rain. The croaking was always at its worst just before dark, and the alleys reverberated with the twittering roar of innumerable toads. I looked up to my balcony as I crossed the street and saw the lace curtains, yellowed from the lamp beside my bed, fluttering in the evening breeze: Lola was waiting for me.

Hungry for all the details of the mayor's symposium, she oohed over every sententious phrase I quoted from my notebook, and her dark eyes flashed like storm clouds rent by lightning when I described the great pink hall in which the engineers presented their conclusions. As Lola melted into my arms, my easy sarcasm about the overblown clichés of the politicians and my fervent cynicism about the efficacy of the engineers' solutions yielded, I am ashamed to admit, to a more heroic account of the day's proceedings. Hours later, as she slept contentedly beside me, I savored the oohs and perhaps even the aahs that my history of the founding of the capital would, no doubt, elicit from her sweet lips. I couldn't wait to begin writing it, so I slipped out of her tender embrace, sat at my desk, and using a flashlight to see the paper, scribbled down everything I could recall from my few hours in the vault.

The next morning, I stopped by the office of an editor of a weekly magazine that had occasionally published my work. He gratefully accepted my offer to prepare an account of the mayor's conference; his regular City Hall correspondent was still in traction at the hospital thanks to a nasty spill. I then offhandedly inquired whether the magazine might be interested in a series of articles on the founding of the city. Because it was summer and a slow time for news, he agreed to a three-part series.

Thus armed with press credentials, I caught a taxi to City Hall and carefully strode into the Office of the Clerk of Public Records to apply for a pass to the city archives. I knew better than to fill out the appropriate forms, which would have languished unread and unapproved for eternity in some eddy of the municipality's torpid and meandering bureaucratic stream. Instead, using one of the many paper clips that were scattered everywhere in City Hall for this very purpose, I attached two examples of our colorful national currency to the back of my press credentials and handed them to the clerk's assistant. The elderly gentleman discreetly palmed the smaller of the two bills as he presented my credentials to his superior. When the papers were returned to me a few moments later, the other bill had been transformed into the pass I desired.

I was directed by a guard to a narrow staircase and descended to the Office of the Municipal Archivist, who peremptorily refused to honor my pass. Displaying some foresight, I had filled one of my pockets with paper clips while waiting in the first clerk's office. Now I was able to attach to the pass a token of my regard for the archivist's important work. Reexamining my authorization, he relented and generously decided to overlook the missing signatures, which he had insisted were essential to its validation.

I wandered about the archives for the better part of an hour, looking for the door to my secret storehouse of history. I vainly checked every door in the place. In exasperation, I returned to the main office, where the archivist was enjoying a small lunch. Careful not to reveal the true object of my search, I wondered where materials about the founding of the city might be kept, early records or a chronicle of some sort, perhaps. At the mention of the word "chronicle," the old man put down his sandwich. Visibly nervous, he told me that all the early records had burned in the great fire. Having gone to college in the old provincial capital, I knew that the great fire to which he alluded had occurred in that city years before the present capital was established. When I corrected him, he hemmed and hawed a bit before explaining that there had been a fire in the archives some years ago, which fortunately had not spread to the rest of the building; however, all the early records of the city had been destroyed. I could tell he was trying to judge whether I believed him. I did my best to assure him that I had been completely taken in by his lie.

I waited in a café across the street for an hour or so, nursing a coffee and trying to fathom the archivist's reaction, before I returned to City Hall, slipped into the great hall, and followed the graffiti-emblazoned corridor back to Suarez y Vallejo and the little room he guarded.

Lowering myself through the opening, I felt against the wall until my hand found the light switch. I opened the mysterious door just a crack and discovered, in the sputtering light, that the entrance to the room had been walled up. The plaster seemed fresh, perhaps a few months old.

I closed the door and leaned against it. I realized I had stumbled upon some mystery involving city officials, but I squeezed the questions out of my head and took down the first volume of the chronicles. Though the books were enormous, the elegant script of the friars was quite large itself, and so I was able to read through the history fairly rapidly. On the other hand, my eyes tired in the flickering light, and my careful notes, executed in the cramped room as I sat on a rough stool before an empty shelf, took time. By the end of the day, I had worked through two volumes.

As I leaned back against the mahogany bench on the streetcar home, I reviewed my notes. In the earliest encounters, the friars had found the Indians totally unpredictable, sometimes lavishing hoards of fruit and game upon the missionaries, other times flaying the skin from quivering Spanish bodies as if it were a great joke. The founding of the new capital, however, provided a fortress from which the prose-lytizers could make forays among the savages under the watchful

pikes and muskets of Spanish infantry. Within a year of the establish-
ment of the city, the local Indians had withdrawn deep into the
forests, abandoning their ancient villages to the jaguars, monkeys, and
frogs. In fact, the first reference to a "Lost Empire" occurred in a
description of the sudden exodus of a local tribe that the missionaries
thought had been converted. One young warrior, separated from the
tribe and detained by the colonial militia, confessed to the priests that
the village had fled because their shamans had prophesied the return
of the emperor. Under the too vigorous questioning of the authorities, the Indian prematurely entered paradise before anything could be
learned of this unnamed monarch.

The next morning, I joined the early flood of secretaries and assis-
tants who preceded their supervisors to work each day at City Hall. In
my briefcase, I carried a sandwich and a jar of juice for lunch as well as
a new lightbulb. I worked until dark without interruption.

By the end of the week, I had covered nearly the first quarter century of the chronicles. The story was fascinating. Jungles were burned
to expand overburdened fields in order to feed the growing population
of the new capital. The sandy soil of the jungle, though, was unfit for
more than a few seasons of plantings, so more of the forest had to be
razed each year. Game retreated so deep into the jungle that monkey
was the only meat available to the city. However, even that source of
food was soon depleted by the unquenchable demand of the new capital. An increasing desperation colored the prose of the successive
priests who narrated the history of these early years. And with growing frequency, references to the returning emperor troubled both sec-
ular and religious authorities throughout this period.

As I sat at the bar of a chic restaurant that Friday night sipping a
martini and waiting for Lola, I regretted the weekend. I was anxious
to see how the administration would respond to the inevitable famine
toward which the young community lurched with its shortsighted
agricultural policies. Also, the recurring mystery of unexplained dis-
appearances of citizens on the outskirts of town, often in broad daylight, had nearly panicked the populace. But most of all, I wanted to

learn more about the "plague" of which the chroniclers complained with growing concern.

Lola, radiant in a white linen dress, was cranky. We had had to forgo our afternoons, and she felt unappreciated. Hoping to surprise her with my project, I foolishly evaded her demands for an explanation of where I was spending my days. Though I would have preferred to use the weekend revising my notes, I devoted most of Saturday and all of Sunday to spoiling my Lola.

We took advantage of a break in the rains Sunday afternoon to visit the zoo, where I noticed something peculiar. As we strolled along the slippery paths from cage to cage, holding tightly to each other, I noticed toads in every crevice, in every paper cup that littered the ground, in every muddy puddle. What was strange, though, was the animals' reactions to the toads. Surely the lions and elephants and bears and giraffes had grown accustomed to the croaking amphibians, but for some reason the animals retreated from the toads, nervously swishing their tails and backing away indignantly from the ugly little creatures. Lola, tossing peanuts to the monkeys that stretched their slender arms through the bars, bubbled with happiness. But as I studied the almost human paws that strained toward us, I fell into a kind of melancholy, which I could not explain and which even the fervent caresses of my beloved, later that night, could not dissipate.

Monday and Tuesday, I doggedly pursued my research, resisting the urge to leap forward among the chronicles out of fear that such knowledge might prejudice my reading of the preceding years. Rumors of the emperor's return circulated widely, I learned as I picked up where I had left off on Friday, despite official decrees from the colonial administration and ecclesiastical condemnations of the legend as a godless superstition. Though the troubling rumors persisted, the authorities and the citizenry at least were comforted by the discovery of the mutilated corpse of one of those who had disappeared just outside the city; what was left of the body provided grisly evidence that the unfortunate had fallen victim to an Indian raiding party, whose stealth in the wild made them nearly invisible. The city celebrated the extinction of at least one of the mysteries that had tormented its sleep by authorizing its militia to embark on a savage campaign against any tribes of the forest that could be found.

By late Wednesday afternoon, I had reached the leather-bound chronicle just prior to the missing volume. But when I reshelved the mangy book about 8:30, I had discovered nothing anticipating events that the current administration might wish to suppress. The circumstances of the early capital were desperate, but no more desperate than they had been the year before, or even the year before that. Exhausted, I switched off the light and made my way home.

Skipping supper, I collapsed into my bed, still dressed, and nodded off. I had been asleep just ten minutes when the phone startled me awake.

It was Lola. She had been waiting for me at the restaurant for an hour—I had completely forgotten our date for that night. I offered to rush right over, but she pouted that it was too late, that I obviously had more important things to do. Still groggy, I let her hang up. It occurred to me that I should take a taxi to her apartment and wait to apologize, but the next thing I knew, the dreary light of dawn was seeping into the room. I had fallen back asleep.

In my rumpled suit, I hurried down the stairs and out into the street. Neither a trolley nor a taxi was in sight, so I began to run toward Lola's, falling twice on the slippery sidewalks. By the time I reached her apartment, the city was stretching awake. Already to the east, clouds were banking up over the rooftops, damping the early light. I leapt up her broad staircase, catching myself on the railing just as my feet slipped out from underneath me. On the landing, a squat toad, corroded with warts, watched me through narrowed eyes.

Stepping around the indifferent beast, I knocked gently at Lola's door. As I was about to knock again, I heard the bolt ease from its buckle, and the door opened wide enough for me to see her disheveled bed behind her, where a man with a mustache lifted himself up on one arm.

Lola was unrepentant. If I could take a new mistress, she insisted, then she could take a new lover. When I protested that there was no other woman, she scoffed and slammed the door in my face. Shaken, I took a step backward and tumbled halfway down the stairs. As I pulled myself up on the banister and stood uncertainly, testing my legs, the toad on the landing began to croak.

I limped to City Hall, indifferent to the deluge that soaked me to the bone. Nodding to the guards who had begun to greet me each morning, I followed the corridors to the great hall. To my distress, the entrance was locked; I had arrived too early. I spent the next hour in a nearby café, drinking hot chocolate and reading the paper. I probably should have gone home and changed, but I knew what gnawing memories lurked in my room—the lace curtains, the bed, even the tub. And to be honest, despite Lola's cruel infidelity, I was still very curious about the mystery of the missing volume.

When I finally found my way to the tiny cell where I had spent the last two weeks, I set immediately to work on the chronicle that followed the missing year. A crabbed, unfamiliar handwriting greeted me on the first page. The awkward scribe, opening with an invocation, prayed that God might preserve the struggling community from another such year as it had just endured. As I read on, the history of the missing twelve months began to emerge in the friar's vague allusions to the pestilence that had decimated the population, the loss of faith that had attended the sudden deaths of so many, the rebellion against both civil and clerical authority that—the merciful Lord be praised—had been suppressed, the unremitting storms that a just God had unleashed upon the town in punishment of its rebellious sins, and the second plague, which had arrived with the rains.

It was clear enough. Considering the multitude of jaundiced corpses that have swelled our cemeteries over the centuries since the city's founding, the first plague was surely yellow fever. And could the second, arriving with the rains, be anything other than a plague of toads? Why else would the current administration, having absconded with the chronicle of that ancient and terrible year, go so far to conceal their crime as to wall up the tiny room in which the Franciscan histories had moldered for hundreds of years? What else might link the destiny of our modern metropolis to that first desperate and ragged colony from which we descended but those slimy amphibians that jeopardized the reelection of all our politicians? It had to be toads.

As the new chronicler dutifully maintained the daily record into the summer months, his prose relaxed a bit, revealing a mischievous sense of humor that sometimes verged on satire. But even his timid little jokes about official malfeasance came as a shock to me: having endured, in the earlier volumes, three decades of pious defense of every cruelty and stupidity visited upon the local populace by civil and ecclesiastical authorities, I was stunned to read my gentle friar's comic denunciation of even Suarez y Vallejo's lechery and avarice.

As the year softened into autumn, his humor turned, at times, almost bitter. By early winter, I began to recognize in the increasingly erratic script of his disjointed sentences the descent of a mind into madness. Over and over again, he described the "Ceremony of Restitution," as he called it. To be honest, I must admit that it read like the hallucination of a fevered brain. The authorities, resplendent in their polished armor and colorful liturgical garb, had marched in a grand procession into the bowels of the earth, a choir of Indian boys leading the way with sacred hymns. Why? My poor, demented little friar insisted that, to forestall greater catastrophes, Suarez y Vallejo had been forced to return to the "emperor" his treasure hoard. "Thus did we save ourselves," he would invariably conclude and close with the moral exhortation "Be not greedy of filthy lucre."

Though the danger had passed—whatever it was—the writer could not escape its terror. Turning a page, I was surprised to find the hand of another priest, who began his watch by lamenting the loss to the community of his predecessor. If I understood the flowery expressions and scriptural allusions of the new scribe correctly, my mad friar had disappeared one winter night, apparently fleeing into the jungle to present himself to the emperor and beg for mercy (or so he had confided to a half-addled scullery servant earlier that evening). Saddened, I closed the old book and laid my face against the chapped grain of its leather.

I did not have the heart to continue; the tragic fate of the little friar had touched me. I realized, all at once, how much I missed my Lola. Resolving to apologize to her for the misunderstanding that I had allowed to crop up between us, promising myself to suppress the pangs of jealousy that had tormented me all day, I gathered up my things, replaced on its shelf the sad story of the mad priest, and hurried off to Lola's apartment. The rain, mercifully, had slackened during the afternoon, and as I waited for my trolley beneath trees whose leaves still bowed under the weight of swollen, trembling raindrops, the city enjoyed the rare pleasure of a rosy, if somewhat murky, sunset. It was a good omen, I told myself.

It did not worry me when, two hours later, Lola had still not yet floated up the steps to the landing where I hunched beside her door. She had girlfriends; perhaps they had all gone to dinner and then decided to catch a movie. Or maybe she was just working late. But by the time her neighbors had returned from walking their dogs and taking out their garbage, by the time their teenagers had sneaked in from illicit rendezvous with boyfriends, and certainly by the time I woke in the middle of the night still huddled against her door, I realized Lola wasn't coming home. I knew, of course, in whose bed she was sleeping that night. But I did not know where the pig with the sleazy mustache kept his sty, so I trudged home through the drizzling dark, desolate.

If my heart had been scraped raw already that night by the rough scapular of my devotion to the woman I loved, imagine the salt in which it was rubbed when I found tacked to my door (by the jeweled hat pin I had given her for Easter) Lola's bitter, tear-stained note. Like me, she had waited all evening, desperate to salvage our love. But when hour succeeded lonely hour late into the night, visions of my infidelity with some new mistress began to provoke her fury. She had given vent to her jealousy in the wounded, merciless prose of her little note. The scrap of paper made clear that I would not find her at home should I try to fabricate some outlandish excuse. The captain—so the pig had a rank, I discovered—had offered her his hospitality. By the time I read this, she wrote coldheartedly, she would already be in his arms, reciprocating his generosity. I sank down onto the floor, aware of the malevolent irony of the whole wretched affair, and did not bother even to kick away the little toads that hopped onto my shoes.

In those touring French farces that had so often entertained the capital when I was a young man, such misunderstandings between lovers merely concluded a frantic fourth act. As the curtain fell on the petulant young woman and her bungling Pierrot, the audience settled back into their red velvet seats, secure in their anticipation of a fifth act that would unravel the knotty confusions that had separated the sweethearts. But this was no farce—at least no theatrical farce. No fifth act would follow. Our romance would not be revived.

With Lola lost to me, hopeless and exhausted, I slept until noon. I rose, disheveled, still wearing the clothes I had put on two days before. Cursing the obsession with those ridiculous chronicles that had cost me my Lola, I drew a bath. The water plunging into the tub from its faucet outroared the rain, which on this darkest afternoon of the summer seemed merely to ooze out of the clouds like—forgive my sentimentality—tears.

But after a hearty lunch and two or three glasses of a rough red wine at a nearby café, I began to be troubled not by memories of Lola but by something my crazy Franciscan had written a few days before he fled into the jungle. "All for a pallet of gold," as I remembered it, "and a casket of emeralds." Racing through his story, I hadn't thought much of the phrase. The sentences of the chronicles were so inflated by the gongoristic rhetoric of the day that I had dismissed the expression as a mere metaphor for the greed condemned so vehemently by the mad priest. Now, though, I recalled how straightforward his earlier accounts had been, how shockingly direct, as a matter of fact. I wondered whether he might have quite literally meant "a pallet of gold and a casket of emeralds." Surely the "Ceremony of Restitution" must have returned something, somewhere, to someone. Could it not have been the gold and emeralds? But where would it have been returned, and to whom?

A fourth glass of wine opened my eyes. The majestic procession had marched "into the bowels of the earth." Of course, I thought.

Falling three times along the way, I rushed back to City Hall and then down the corridor to my secret room. But when I came to the faded portrait of Suarez y Vallejo, I did not stop. Instead, I began to run along the ill-lit ramp that seemed to circle down to the very heart of the earth. Then, slowing suddenly in the increasingly narrow spiral, I caught myself with both hands as I ran into the blank wall in which the corridor terminated. It was not what I had expected. Breathless, I sat down, my head resting against the wall.

At first I wasn't really aware of it, the thundering, I mean. But as I pressed my ear against the wall, I heard—no, felt—the deep octaves of rumbling thunder on the other side. I began to examine the wall more closely. Even in the dirty light cast by a distant bulb, I recognized the same fresh plaster that had entombed the chronicles in their little cell. The wall was a recent addition to the corridor, perhaps a few months old. I found a rusty iron rod some yards back up the ramp and began to chip away at the plaster.

My tool poked through the few inches of plaster until it struck wood. As I rammed the rod against the obstruction, I heard the echo of my knocking reverberate somewhere nearby. Frightened that I might be discovered, I paused, but no other sound interrupted the low roar on the far side of the wall. I enlarged the hole I had cut and, using the rod as a crowbar, began to crack chunks of plaster loose. As I stood, dusty among the white rubble, an ancient wooden door, girdled in iron, confronted me. A barricade fit to imprison the devil himself, the door was cross-locked with bolts secured by massive locks. Its iron frame was fastened to solid rock, and I realized for the first time that the walls and the roof of the corridor were chiseled stone. Still, the centuries had taken their toll. Here and there, wood worms had threaded tiny tunnels in the oak planks of the door. And, I discovered without surprise, something sharp had scored the years of rust on the great locks with fresh scratches. I put my lips to the largest wormhole and blew the sawdust out. Then, lying on my stomach, I pressed my eye against the little chink.

With what a mixture of terror and wonder did I view the damp cavern behind the door, where thousands, millions of toads bellowed in eerie phosphorescence. Perhaps it was only that I lay face-to-face with them, but their serrated roar struck me as threatening, even belligerent. I jerked away my head as a huge toad hurled itself against the door where I had been spying on them.

The sudden movement of my head woke me with a shudder. The dream had been so vivid, I struggled for a moment in terrifying confusion. Then I saw before me the blank wall where I had sunk down in drunkenness. There was no wooden door, no bellowing toads. And as I looked more closely and began to scrape at the wall with my fingernails, I found that there was not even plaster—just the pale stone from which the entire corridor had been chiseled.

Upon that rock my voyage of discovery seemed on the verge of foundering. My descent into the depths of an ancient riddle had driven me headlong into the implacable, inexorable dead end that is the womb of all mystery. But then, my ears still echoing with the bellow of the toads, I remembered the reverence with which our Indians utter their dreams. And in this matter especially, it occurred to me, ought I not allow myself to be instructed by the children of the forest that we, in our arrogance, had for centuries despoiled? The truth had never before been so obvious to me. Half drunk, I had no trouble convincing myself that I had dreamt no dream. No, I had received—from whom, I dared not consider—a vision, a revelation.

Dusting myself off, I returned to the secret room, hid in my jacket the last chronicle I had read, and nonchalantly escaped with the crowd of bureaucrats that City Hall disgorged for the weekend at five o'clock. Perhaps I was impelled by a broken heart and vainly hoped I might yet win back Lola, perhaps it was an act of homage to the little Franciscan driven mad by the avarice of the authorities, perhaps I really believed myself the prophet of a forgotten god, but by Monday morning as I sat in the editorial offices of the weekly magazine that had commissioned my series on the founding of the city, I had written an exposé that would be excoriated by the mayor as "scurrilous," by his chief adviser as "groundless," and by even the poor municipal archivist as "totally fabricated."

And they were right, of course. But the unrelenting rain and the profusion of toads drowned out their denials. My story, full of superstition and legend, satisfied the deep-seated belief of many of my fellow citizens that the supernatural was the only reasonable explanation of our current predicament. To couple such superstition with the all-too-likely charge that corrupt politicians had precipitated the crisis through their greed was to insure broad support for my exposé.

Of course, nothing came of it. First of all, the state prosecutors were all members of the mayor's party. Similarly, I later wheedled from the municipal archivist the admission that, having drawn the mayor's attention to the worrisome parallels between the plague depicted in the chronicles and our own "situation," as he put it, he had been persuaded by the mayor, to the everlasting shame of both the archivist and his profession, to destroy the missing volume to keep it from precipitating a panic among the public; however, the confession failed to appear in print after the owner of my weekly magazine was honored by the president with a lifetime appointment as a deputy minister without portfolio.

And, after all, there was no sacred cave beneath City Hall. Even if they had wanted to end the rain and drive out the toads with a second Ceremony of Restitution, neither the pallet of gold nor the casket of emeralds—mere figures of speech, I now realize—could be restored by a state procession to the emperor's green cavern.

So the authorities scoffed at my allegations. They even declined to prosecute me for removing municipal property from City Hall, though I was made to return the volume—a final betrayal of the mad priest, I thought.

The rain continued. The toads' slime, we came to learn, grew more and more toxic with each exposure.

The children were the first to be sent away. Then the pregnant women and the aged. Finally the mayor declared that he would follow in the footsteps of our national hero, Suarez y Vallejo, and move the capital to a more hospitable locale. And so, eventually, the last of them hobbled away on their crutches and canes, even my dark delicious Lola and her mustachioed captain.

As for me, I found I could not exile myself so easily. I, too, it is true, abandoned the city, traveling widely, both on the continent and elsewhere. The years flowed like rainwater swelling a gutter, but like the little Franciscan, I could not put behind me the events that had transpired in the capital during that damp summer so many years ago. The emperor, I continued to believe, deserved reparations. I determined to return.

Only the intervention of my doctors, who have inconvenienced me for so long in this foreign asylum, prevents my repatriation. They dispute my claims. They stubbornly maintain that no records can be found of a capital abandoned in this century. They torment me with their accusations that I cannot even remember the name of the city of my birth or of the country to which I continue to pledge my allegiance. (Forget those names? I would more likely forget my own name. No, I simply decline to provide any information that might lead to the renewed exploitation of my little country, my beloved city.) They parade before me strangers, pretending to be my relatives. A ridiculous old woman—my aunt, she swears—insists that I was born here in Philadelphia. That I grew up in Germantown. That I studied at Penn. Mistaken identity, I explain sympathetically. But the woman is senile; she calls me Morris and will not be dissuaded.

So I now appeal in writing for my freedom. I have laid out for you the whole story. Who could believe that I have invented all this—and in such telling detail? Will you continue to require me to accept the old woman's fiction as the price of my liberty? I cannot. I have suffered so much for its sake that I could never betray the truth.

And so, I sit here in my little cell, pen in hand, as if in that other cramped cell half a world away, as if hunched over the final blank page of the last volume of the ecclesiastical chronicle of the first century (and now, thanks to my doggedness, of the final months as well) of a once great capital, writing by candlelight of a city that no longer exists, for people who have been scattered like leaves before a great whirlwind, while overhead the abandoned buildings, long since reclaimed by the patient jungle, echo with the thunder of a multitude of small, hoarse voices, croaking in the dark for their emperor, who, aloof as always, disdains even now to show himself to his faithful subjects.

Fatherhood

THEIR ROMANCE WAS still in its first flower when Sami, after a long and moody evening, weepily admitted to Steven that she was pregnant with his child. He comforted her as best he could.

That night, as she lay asleep in the bed they shared, Steven stared at Sami in the dark. He tried to imagine what was happening inside her. But even more intently he tried to imagine what would happen inside himself in seven or eight months when a squalling, bloody infant emerged from the swollen womb and a nurse offered the newborn to him.

By morning, Steven had resolved to marry Sami. He found himself incapable of abandoning the woman in the midst of her pregnancy. Nor was he willing to capitulate to his fears by suggesting an abortion or any other expedient: after their discussion the night before, he had no doubt that Sami wanted this child. And he, after all, wanted Sami.

Returning from their brief honeymoon, the couple began to transform themselves into parents. The expectant mother scrubbed down the apartment, rooting out grime from corners Steven had somehow overlooked and teasing out stains that had blemished his walls for years. Mangy carpets, worn down to nubs of illegible design, were shoved out the window by lazy rag collectors as Steven hovered about the room, fretting over their indifference. But he never objected to Sami's renovation of his apartment. Even when the disabled veterans maneuvered his old rolltop desk down the stairs and into their truck, he did not protest his new wife's wishes to turn the study into a nursery. He readily agreed with her that "the baby has to sleep somewhere." In fact, he came home early one evening to help her paper the walls of the new bedroom with a bright pattern of seashells and fish and sailboats. Finishing at midnight, the couple admired their work. Sami hugged Steven. "I can't remember ever being this happy before," she said, starting to cry.

It was the next morning when the bleeding began.

Steven was buffeting between sleep and the daylight that flooded the windows over the bed when he heard Sami's weak call from the bathroom. Standing in front of the shut door, frightened, he asked her what was wrong. "There's blood," she said in a quivering voice. At first, he didn't understand what she meant, but when she opened the door, the way she slowly shook her head back and forth explained everything to him.

"No," he insisted, "it's going to be OK."

Sami wouldn't look at him. She just kept shaking her head. "Something's wrong."

"You lie down. We'll call the doctor."

The doctor told Sami to stay in bed with her feet elevated. "This is not uncommon," he assured her.

But the spotting, as the physician called it, continued. Though restless, Sami followed the doctor's orders, passing whole days in bed. Steven, distressed over her confinement, dragged the television into the bedroom and even rented a portable refrigerator, which he set on the night table. Hurrying home at the end of the day from the men's shop where he worked as a salesclerk, he stopped at the newsstand on the corner to gather magazines for her, at the laundry to pick up fresh bed linens, at the Korean grocery across the street to choose meat and vegetables for their dinner as well as a little bouquet of mixed carnations to cheer her up. He even braved the occasional child in the sweetshop to bring home red licorice, Sami's secret weakness.

The couple fell into a cozy routine, nibbling their meals together in bed, playing cards or working on crossword puzzles, reading the paper, watching old movies. Like every happy man, Steven began to imagine that the sea upon which he drifted was infinite, unbounded by the ragged shoals and craggy beaches upon which he would soon founder. And so it was with genuine surprise that he woke to Sami's sobs one night and found the sheets awash in blood.

Though the doctor pronounced the woman perfectly fit, Steven imagined a pallor in her cheeks, a weakness in her voice in the days following her miscarriage. Finding her at the window watching little girls on the sidewalk below play hopscotch, he sensed her melancholy and blamed the lost child.

The man knew it was absurd, but even as Sami's mood brightened over the next few weeks, he recognized a simmering anger he could not suppress. Worried by its tenacity, Steven had nearly convinced himself to make an appointment with Dr. Bernard, his old therapist, when he first saw the child in the nursery.

Although Sami seemed to have put the pregnancy behind her, she had not yet been able to bring herself to pack up the bassinet draped in yellow bunting, the painted music box around which cantered a sly calico cat steadily pursuing three white mice, the rocking chair with its decals of twined roses, and the few other furnishings in the nursery. Steven thought it would be a kindness to remove to the apartment's storage bin in the basement these poignant reminders of her loss. So one Saturday afternoon, he sent his wife off shopping while he stayed home, he told her, to fix the leaking kitchen faucet.

Opening the door that the couple had kept closed for weeks, Steven was surprised at how much colder than the rest of the apartment the room had grown. The day's winter light already had started to thicken toward darkness, and the wallpaper's gay sailboats and frolicking fish danced over a pale ocean that shimmered with golden shadows. Suddenly, as he turned from the wall, Steven saw the child standing unsteadily before the window.

Though he felt his throat tightening, he was more annoyed than startled. The boy or girl—he could not tell which in the heavy coat and stocking cap from which the child peeked out—seemed simply curious in regarding him. Steven managed to wheeze, "What are you doing here?" But even before the words were out, the small figure had disappeared.

The child had looked so real, so fleshy bundled in coat and mittens and cap, the thought had not occurred to Steven that it might be a mere hallucination. He walked to the window. No drops of water beaded on the wooden floor where the little red snow boots had stood. He did not know what to think. Leaving the bassinet untouched, he closed the door. By the time Sami returned with an armful of bargains an hour later, he had changed the washer in the faucet.

Though the child troubled him, Steven, of course, said nothing to his wife. It was a memory, he explained to himself, really a piece of a memory that had somehow slipped out inadvertently. It was a waking dream. But all his explanations collapsed beneath him later that night.

Rising from bed after Sami had fallen asleep, Steven tiptoed down the hall to the nursery. He had felt almost compelled to get up and check the room again. It was with the most exacting patience that he turned the doorknob until, like an overwound clock, it resisted further winding. He pushed the door open with a sudden jerk and heard the knob uncoil like a spring. The window, its curtains still open, glowed from streetlights and the neon signs of the shops below. Over his shoulder, the sconce on the wall in the hallway cast its feeble yellow shadow over the floor. He didn't need to flip on the room's own light to know the child was not there. The room was empty.

Then, just as he allowed himself a deep breath, he heard the whimpering. His first thought was that Sami was crying, but in the next instant he knew it was somewhere in the nursery. Following the choked-back sobbing to the closet, Steven hesitated only a moment before gently swinging open the door. The sound was at his feet, he knew, though he could see nothing. He reached up for the beaded chain to the light. As it flashed on, the wrenching, hopeless weeping was extinguished. Steven fell to his knees, running his fingers over the closet's oak floorboards. When he held up his hands, they were tipped with nothing but dust.

The next day, anxious to leave the apartment, he took Sami on a walk. The afternoon was beautiful, the banked snow glistening beneath a brisk blue sky. Though he tried to steer clear of the park on the way home—overrun, as it would be on such a day, with young parents and their babies—his wife insisted, and they found a bench in the sun. Across the walk, young children played on merry-go-rounds and slides, monkey bars and swings. Steven shifted uncomfortably as he sought among the bright snowsuits some hint of the child he had seen the day before, the child he was sure he had heard the night before, in the nursery. There was one, from the back, who caught his attention, but when the little girl turned around he realized there was no resemblance. Another, crying, made him look twice. In the end, though, none of the children reminded him of the child he was seeking. As the park's elms began to stipple the bench in chilly shadows, Steven helped Sami up and suggested they get something hot to drink.

Taking little sips of the café's bitter coffee, Sami kept adding sugar, one packet after another. Steven smiled at her fondly. "Are you very sad?" he asked. "About the baby, I mean."

"I feel like a different person," she said quietly. "A year ago, before I met you, it was like I was floating, like a boat drifting down the river."

"And now?" he wondered.

"And now . . . ," she whispered hoarsely, but she was already crying before she could say another word. She reached across the table and took his hand.

A week passed before he opened the nursery door again. Having just gotten home from work, Steven had gone to the bedroom to change out of his suit. As he walked down the hall back to the kitchen, where Sami was running the water, cleaning spinach for dinner, he stopped in front of the nursery and peeked in. The child, in green coveralls, was crouched over some toys in the dark. Steven watched as the little head turned toward the door, and their eyes met. Then there was nothing there, nothing more than moonlight and neon frosting the windowpanes. He closed the door.

His silence at dinner worried Sami; she wanted to know what was bothering him. He was about to lie to her when he heard himself say, "There's a child in the nursery."

Sami's face paled. "What?"

"A child," he said, too embarrassed to look up from his dinner.

"What child?"

"Not a child, not really a child." He was fumbling for the right word. "A figment, something, a hallucination."

Sami stared at him.

"I don't know, something." He wanted to convince her. "It was there last week, and now it's back."

Without a word, she got up from the table. Steven listened to her heels clacking along the hall, her hand twisting the doorknob, the hinges grating as they swung back on themselves. He even heard the light click on and then, a few moments later, click off.

Sami's chair scraped against the floor when she sat down again. "There's no one there," she said angrily, "nothing."

Steven wanted desperately for her to believe him. "Last Saturday night, it was crying. After you went to sleep."

"Why are you doing this?"

That night they slept with their backs to each other, Steven staring into the darkness as he listened to his wife's soft weeping.

When he returned from work the next evening, he found Sami at the kitchen table. Her head was in her hands.

"I'm sorry. I'm so sorry," he said as he bent to kiss her.

But the woman interrupted him. "I saw the child," she whispered in a voice that made him tremble. "In the nursery."

He sank down onto a chair beside her.

"On the window seat, looking out." She was silent for a moment. "Then it saw me . . . and disappeared."

"I'm sorry, sweetheart," Steven sighed, taking her hand.

Sami looked at her husband. A tear slid down her cheek. "When I went to the window, I saw what the child was looking at." She took a deep breath. "The two little girls from across the street. They were playing on their stoop."

Steven was taken aback. "It was watching other children?"

Biting her lip, Sami simply nodded.

"We have to move," her husband decided even as he spoke. "We'll stay at a hotel tonight."

"No!" Sami objected. "We can't abandon that baby. It needs us."

"You're just upset. We'll go to the Randolph; it's not too expensive. Then tomorrow we'll decide what to do."

"No," she insisted, "we're staying here. It needs us."

"How do you know it needs us? It's not even real. It's just . . . just a . . ."

"Just a what?" Sami interrupted. "That child is so sad. We're not leaving it here alone."

Steven recognized a determination in his wife's voice that he had never heard before. "All right," he nodded, "we'll stay if that's what you want. But don't go back in there—not without me, at least."

They waited until after dinner before they took each other's hand and opened the nursery door. The child, in flannel pajamas printed with a design they could not quite make out in the dim light, lay on the floor. When they came in, it sat up and looked at them. Then, to their surprise, they saw its lips move, though they heard nothing.

"Oh, Steven, do you see?" Sami whispered. "It wants to tell us something."

Her husband flicked on the light. The vision vanished in the flash of illumination. Frozen in sudden incandescence, the useless furnishings of the room seemed steeped in melancholy.

"Why did you do that? You made it go away."

"I thought we might see better," he lied.

All the next day, Steven tried to convince himself that his wife would come to understand they had to move, to start over somewhere else, but when he came home that evening, he found her in the darkened nursery, sitting in the rocking chair. She smiled at her husband and, as he started to speak, put a finger to her lips, nodding toward the corner of the room. Among the thickening shadows, the man saw something move.

Steven slept restlessly that night, as he had the night before. Just after midnight, drowsing in and out of a dream he could not quite remember, he thought he heard singing. Then—he wasn't sure how long later—Sami jostled him from sleep as she slipped back underneath the blanket. "It's all right," she whispered, "sound asleep." Steven was awake now. "Just like an angel."

She leaned over and kissed him. Steven put his arm under her head and began to kiss her neck. He expected her to tauten, to lean away. They had not made love since the bleeding had begun, weeks and weeks ago. But she pulled him closer, already fumbling with the buttons of his pajamas. The two of them yielded to ferocious desire.

At breakfast, Steven almost expected a quarrel. He began to apologize even before she turned from the stove as he walked into the kitchen. But she was singing the song, a lullaby he suddenly realized, that he had heard the night before. He had forgotten what she looked like when she was happy. *This is wrong*, he thought to himself.

Sami called him on his lunch break. "The baby is moody today," she worried over the phone. "Baby?" he repeated, at first not grasping to whom she referred.

He did not come straight home that evening. Stopping in a coffee shop near work, he stared into the blackness of his cup and tried to make sense of what was happening to them.

"Oh, Steven," the woman exclaimed when he unlocked the front door. She had been waiting for him in the living room.

He started to make an excuse about being late, but she interrupted him.

"Its lips, Steven, I know what they were trying to say." Her eyes were glistening with tears.

To calm her, he took her hands and made her sit on the sofa.

" 'Mama.' I think it was trying to say 'Mama.' "

The man groaned. "It's not real, Sami. I don't know what it is, but it's not a child."

"Oh, it is, Steven. It is a child. And it needs us," she insisted.

Steven shook his head and sighed. "Or maybe we need it."

"What difference does it make? We're a family now."

Steven's mouth turned sour. "Family?" he repeated, swallowing hard against the nausea already searing the back of his throat.

He let Sami chatter gaily through dinner about the child, but he had already made up his mind. *It's for her own good,* he told himself, though he felt like a murderer whose victim, unaware of his intentions, was confiding in him her happy plans for a future she would not have.

The solution was simple, of course. The miscarried baby, he had finally understood that evening, was like a star that had collapsed into itself. And even though there was nothing left but emptiness, they were being drawn into it, into that tiny, dark heart of emptiness. Only one thing could pull them free of its merciless gravity. Though his wife did not realize it, they had, the night before, already begun to save themselves, he reminded himself to assuage his guilt.

Late that night, Sami awoke among the tangled sheets, still damp with pleasure, and found that Steven was not in the bed. She put her nightgown back on and felt her way down the dark hall to the nursery. Gently opening the door, she saw her husband in the light of the window, rocking slowly in her chair.

"What's wrong?" she whispered. "Is it the baby?"

Steven sighed. "Come here, sweetheart."

The woman sat in his lap, her head on his shoulder.

"There is no baby, Sami. We're just pretending. And it's my fault. I'm the one who started all this."

"Yes, you're the father. But the baby is real. I don't know how, but it is."

The man ignored her assurance. "You were so unhappy, I guess I just wanted to comfort you. I came in here to put everything away, and thinking about you and hearing the kids outside . . ."

Sami was patting his chest. "It's all right. You don't have to explain. It doesn't matter how it happened. But now the baby is ours."

Steven was exasperated. "There is no baby. It's only wishful thinking, regret. That's all it is, a wish we twisted into a shadow."

He could feel her shaking her head. "You think it's just some kind of dream of what might have been, but it's more than that."

"It doesn't matter what it is," he said, almost angrily. "As soon as you get pregnant again, it will fade away. You'll see."

She looked up into his face. "But I can't get pregnant."

"Of course, you can. The doctor said you were perfectly fine."

"No." She smiled. "You can't get pregnant when you're nursing."

Once again Steven winced with the disquieting fear that had troubled him the last three days. "You're not nursing, Sami."

She did not answer him. Instead, she slipped the strap of her gown off one shoulder, exposing her breast. Her hand played with the nipple until she lifted a finger to his lips. His tongue recoiled from the too sweet, thin taste of warm milk.

Coming home from work the next evening and not finding Sami in the kitchen, Steven fruitlessly searched the apartment. He was worried about her. Perhaps he would find her asleep in the bedroom, taking a nap. Or maybe, he realized with a sigh, she was in the nursery. But the bed was unwrinkled, and the rocking chair was empty. She had gone to the grocery, he decided. So when she emerged from the hall, a few minutes later, he was taken aback.

"Where were you?" he demanded.

"Playing with the baby," she said with a quizzical look.

"That's impossible. I checked the nursery when I came home. You weren't there."

She filled a pot with water. "Sure I was," she insisted, "in the rocking chair. Feeding the baby."

Steven did not pursue the matter. But two nights later, waking without Sami in the bed, he again found the apartment empty when he searched. Trying the nursery a second time, though, he discovered Sami asleep on the floor beneath the nursery window, the child nestled in her arms.

When he tried to understand what was happening to them, Steven persisted in the image of orbiting spheres: two planets following different paths, sometimes beside each other, sometimes blocked from the other's view by the child—he no longer bothered to debate the word—around which they spun. Now, though, he began to fear that Sami's orbit was decaying, spiraling slowly toward the tiny black hole that whipped them along their circuits. To save his wife, he had somehow to counterbalance its drag upon her, to stabilize her distance between child and husband.

Each day when he called on his break, he began to ask Sami how the baby was doing. He could hear in her bubbly descriptions of the morning's activities her relief that Steven's resistance to the idea of the child was wilting. And for the first time, he brought home a toy.

"Oh, Stevie will love this," Sami exclaimed, shaking the bright rattle next to her ear.

"Stevie?"

"He's his father's son." She smiled indulgently.

Steven did not object; he knew he was winning his wife's trust and was confident he could wean her, little by little, from the child.

He fixed an elaborate meal the next weekend for Sami, even deploying the pair of silver candlesticks they had received as a wedding gift and remembering a bouquet of crocuses, her favorite flower, for the table. Distracted by his attentive conversation and silly jokes, she did not mention the baby. Later, lounging on the sofa as she sipped the dregs of the champagne Steven had served with the double-chocolate torte he had baked, the woman let herself be taken by the eager lover.

Afterward, with Sami drowsing in his arms, the man found himself puzzled by the easy assurance with which she had allowed herself to be pleased all evening. He had hesitated, once, twice, half expecting her to take over the serving of the dinner, the cutting of the torte, even the making of love. That had been her habit before the baby. Now, though, she seemed perfectly at ease luxuriating in his attention, sprawled disheveled along the sofa, awaiting his caress. He looked down the length of her body and woke her with his kisses.

Worried, the man continued his paradoxical strategy of humoring Sami even as he sought to distract her from preoccupation with the child. And it seemed to work. Steven did not have to look for her; she was always there, beside him. She had ceased to plead the child's case to her husband. Coming up behind her as she washed the dishes, he now sometimes caught—instead of song—the long whispered breath of a sigh escape her.

Steven took for granted he was winning back his wife. He discovered, though, that he had been humoring only himself when Sami remarked one evening in the nursery how different he seemed to her.

"Different?"

She rocked in the chair; dangling one leg from the window seat, he watched the street shimmer under a glaze of freezing rain. The child was sitting on the floor, its back to them. When the woman spoke, its head turned toward the voice.

"You know, more serious," she said slowly, choosing her words with care, "more here, more—I don't know, just more."

Steven realized she was right: he was different. In fact, he barely recognized in the window his own reflected face, scarred with thick calluses of ice where the sleet had frozen as it trailed down the glass.

Then all at once, staring at himself, he understood his wife had meant not just what she had said but also something else. She was asking in her quiet way whether he really had accepted this delusion playing at her feet, this little madness of theirs, this family.

"It's not real, you know," he sighed.

The room chilled as Steven watched Sami rock, ever so slightly, back and forth. He had not noticed when the pelting storm had softened into snow, but glancing out the window again, he found the world swaddled in white.

The man looked upon his wife and child, and he felt something inside click open—as if a secret lock had been disengaged by small hands that, cupping his heart above and below, had twisted it first one way and then another.

The little creature crawled toward him and batted the cuff of his pants.

What was it, he tried to remember as he lifted up his son, that he had been resisting all this time, that he had always resisted?

The Work of Art

Denn das Schöne ist nichts
als des Schrecklichen Anfang, den wir noch grade ertragen. . . .
—RAINER MARIA RILKE

For Beauty is nothing
but the beginning of terror, which we just barely can still endure. . . .

THE YOUNG MAN, lost in the warren of dingy dentist offices, import companies, and commercial insurance agencies on the eighth floor of the old Effinger Building, was attempting to deliver contracts to a ship chandler. He was sure that the directory beside the florid bronze elevator doors downstairs had listed the chandler in 817. But the last door on the dim hall was 815. He tried the knob. It was locked. He tapped on the milky glass pane with his law school ring just below an arc of golden letters that spelled J. GRUEN.

A thin voice answered his knock. Though the door opened only slightly, the overheated air of the office swarmed over him in the chilly hallway. "I'm looking for Hugo Fernandez, the ship supplier," he explained. "I'm Peter Lagarde. An attorney." He passed his business card to the old man peering at him from behind the door.

"Not on this floor. No Fernandez."

Lagarde looked past the old man into the office. Its walls were covered with paintings.

The thin voice strengthened. "You collect?"

"Collect art? A bit." Lagarde had learned in his four years as an associate at Daigle, Johnson to present a version of himself in matters of taste that might win the confidence of the clients and, especially, of the partners of the firm. He could be quite convincing; as an undergraduate, he had taken a minor in art history. But the small house he had bought and the stocks in which he had invested the proceeds of his trust fund left no capital for speculation in the art market. "Actually," Lagarde continued, "I've been thinking about expanding my collection."

"Perhaps I have something that might interest you." The door swung open.

Lagarde entered the small office, crowded with nineteenth-century portraits and religious works. It had been designed for a secretary; another door opened on a larger second room, where he glimpsed an ornately framed landscape. "Ah, the Impressionists." He was on safe ground; he remembered the movement because he had found its works so painfully absent of interest and so resistant to study for examinations.

"Actually, they're Postimpressionists." The old man pushed farther open the door into the other room. "Here, take a closer look."

Lagarde was surprised: the names of the artists were familiar. "I didn't know there were any galleries in this building," he said.

"Gallery? You call this a gallery? In Philadelphia for thirty years, there I had a gallery. But Hedda dies, God rest her, and my daughter makes me move here to New Orleans. I'm too old to live alone, she says. But I'm not going to retire, am I?"

The young man, half listening, surveyed a group of charcoals above a file cabinet.

"No, I sell what I can get a decent price for, the rest I take with me. Now I peddle masterpieces by phone to cowboys in Oklahoma. But it makes my Sarah happy to have me here, so what can I do?" Even as he talked, he urged his guest toward the drawings with a gentle push. "She makes me crazy, though, that girl. The door I have to keep locked, she says. What kind of business keeps its door locked? Bookies, they keep their door locked."

Lagarde recognized a Degas. He flipped the tag dangling at the bottom of the frame and gasped.

"Don't worry, that was just for the insurance during shipping. I can take ten percent off the top. No problem."

"No, I don't think so. And I've got to find Fernandez. He's expecting these papers."

"Wait. I have something for you." The old man was trying to lift a large, shallow box. Lagarde took the crate from him and put it down on a desk full of magazines. "You like Degas. I can tell. Here is something special. I got it cheap, just before I left Philadelphia."

Gruen had trouble flicking open the rusty latch that fastened the plywood top. "Wait a minute." He took a small hammer from a file cabinet and tapped open the hook. The top creaked back on dry hinges. "This is something a young man would like."

As Lagarde looked down, his breath caught in his throat. A small, exquisite woman gazed up at him from her bath.

"A Degas maquette. It's called *The Tub*. 1889, I think." They both regarded the sculpture. "She's charming, isn't she? I knew you'd like her."

Though the old man wore a cardigan with a high collar that was much too big for him, the musty heat made Lagarde almost dizzy. "How much?" he whispered.

"Let me see." As Gruen lifted the edge of the lead pan that Degas had used as the tub, his bony left hand crawled under like a spider. Slowly it withdrew with a yellow stub dangling a green string. "160,000. But minus the ten percent, it's yours for 144. A steal, let me tell you."

Lagarde was pale. His heart shook his chest.

"If it were a bronze, you couldn't touch it for under 750 these days. But it's wax and plaster. The way Degas is going, I ought to hold on to it. Give it five years, it'll double, triple, who knows? But forget the money. Just look at her."

Lagarde had not taken his eyes off her. She stared up at him over crossed legs, her left foot cupped in her right hand as she lolled in her bath.

"Too much? You could buy on time. By the month."

Her left hand held a sponge. Her hair was like a clump of wet, thick cloth. Lagarde was taking deep, quiet breaths, trying to calm himself. Degas had worked a reddish brown pigment into the wax to resemble bronze; why hadn't he cast the piece? Lagarde guessed without bothering to calculate that he couldn't afford it even if he sold everything: the house, the stocks, the car. "It's very nice, very fine. But I've really got to find Fernandez. It was a pleasure meeting you." Lagarde had already backed into the outer office and was feeling for the door. "Perhaps I'll stop back when I have more time." He closed the door before the old man could speak. His breath burst from him in little white clouds as he hurried down the cold hallway.

As the elevator descended, he leaned against a carved walnut panel. He left the papers for the ship chandler with the guard at the information desk.

＊

PETER LAGARDE busied himself for the next few weeks with a complex lawsuit arising from the grounding of a barge near White Castle in Iberville Parish. He had been accompanied on the site visit by a young Baton Rouge attorney representing some of the underwriters. She was a second-year associate named Lauren and, like him, a graduate of Tulane. The litigation kept them in frequent communication, and among the marine surveys, the depositions, and the motions for summary judgment, a friendship began to emerge. Lagarde found himself scheduling their appointments late in the afternoon so she might be more likely to stay for dinner. He surprised her with symphony tickets one night, but she couldn't stay—she had to prepare for a trial the next morning. He worried over whether he could give her a Christmas present without embarrassing her.

Just before the holidays, an envelope arrived for him at the firm. There was a Canal Street return address. Inside, a photocopied letter from the Gruen Gallery announced a Christmas sale. At the bottom of the letter was a handwritten note: "For tax purposes, I can let you have the Degas for $125,000 until the end of the year." He felt something like panic overtaking him. How had Gruen gotten his address? He remembered the business card he had offered the old man.

In fact, despite his work and despite his colleague from Baton Rouge, he had been unable to force the woman in the tub from his mind. At odd moments, he discovered himself imagining her. He had even spoken with a real estate agent and his broker. After expenses, he could expect $85,000 from the house and his investments. The car was only a year old; he would certainly clear $15,000. He had been relieved to realize that he really couldn't afford the piece. Where would he find $44,000? But now, thanks to Gruen's tax man, he was only $25,000 short, and Lagarde knew where he could find $25,000.

He picked up the phone and called his grandmother. He didn't mention the money. He wished Nana a merry Christmas and told her about his progress at Daigle, Johnson. He hinted at a romance with Lauren. He admitted that he couldn't get away to join his parents in New York for the holidays, but he knew they would understand. Nana insisted that he have Christmas dinner with her at the Wharton; he gracefully accepted.

He was ashamed even before he had hung up. But, he told himself, he wasn't going to ask his grandmother for the money because he wasn't going to buy the Degas. Even if it were the great investment Gruen suggested, it was insane for him to consider buying such a work of art. It would cost him everything he owned, plus a great deal more. And all he would have to show for it was an exquisite lump of wax.

That night, after a quick dinner at a new Mexican restaurant on Magazine, Lagarde stopped by the Tulane library. The reference librarian showed him the registers of prices paid at auction for artworks. Gruen had not exaggerated, but there was nothing like the maquette in the records. He could only guess that the enormous prices fetched by Degas bronzes could make his sculpture worth a quarter of a million in the right auction. Again, for the second time that day, he felt shame. But to his surprise, he realized that he was ashamed of thinking of his little bather in terms of money. He put his hands on the red cover of the closed volume before him and stared at his reflection in the window.

The next morning, Lagarde had coffee with Tommy Hinton, a friend in his firm's business section who specialized in estates. He explained his father wanted to surprise his mother with a fiftieth birthday present, a Degas sculpture. The colleague offered to check it out. "No sweat, we handle stuff like this all the time. You can't imagine the crap we have to do for the old farts we represent. Just get me the papers on it—and the price."

At lunch, he walked over to Gruen's. His heart was beating faster and faster as he rode the current of holiday shoppers. He noticed a legless beggar with a dog in the alcove of a bankrupt department store. The peeling sheets of brown paper revealed glimpses of mannequins in summer smocks; he recalled from his childhood the Christmas window displays of the store.

He pulled his coat closed against the cold, damp gusts. A ragged preacher with a plastic loudspeaker attached to his belt berated the crowds hurrying past. Lagarde tried to avoid the man's attention as he slipped into the Effinger Building.

As the old, ornate elevator creaked toward the eighth floor, he realized that he wouldn't have time for lunch. He was hungry, but this was more pressing.

The door to 815 was ajar. Lagarde peeked in. Gruen and another man were eating sandwiches on a crate. "Come in, come in," the old man insisted, rewrapping his food as he spoke. "This is my neighbor,

Mr. Ruiz. He has the business next door." The lawyer nodded to the small dark man. "You're here for the Degas, am I right?"

"No, not today. I just wanted to ask you a few questions about it."

"Questions? Yes, ask me questions," the old man said, motioning to Ruiz to stay.

"First, could I have a copy of the papers?"

"The papers?"

"You know, to authenticate the piece." Lagarde saw the old man stiffen. "Not that there's any question."

The slightest smile creased Gruen's face. "Of course. I don't buy without papers." He turned to Ruiz and winked. "Well, maybe if it's really cheap, I make an exception."

"You have my address," the attorney reminded him.

"I'll put a copy in the mail this afternoon, no problem," the old man promised, still smiling.

"Also, I was wondering—and I'm not sure I want to go ahead with this—but I was wondering whether you needed all the money by the first of January?"

"December thirty-first. Not January."

Lagarde corrected himself. "Yes, all the money by the end of December?"

"If I wait until January, I may as well wait another year. Taxes. You're a lawyer; you know."

"Midnight on the thirty-first," Ruiz interjected.

"So you need everything?" Lagarde tried one last time.

Gruen shrugged. "Of course everything. If you want to buy on time, then we have to go back to the first price. But come see her again. Look here." The old man had shuffled into the back room and was struggling with the lid of the container.

"No, no, it's not necessary," Lagarde protested, weakening.

"Come, come see."

While Lagarde hesitated, Ruiz got up to view the piece.

"Oh, beautiful," he said with a vague Latin accent. "Look at her. And served up on a platter."

"It's a tub," Lagarde objected as he joined the two men peering into the low crate. The plaster podium of crumpled canvas on which Degas had set the piece swirled with the frozen folds of the cloth, like a woman's robe dropped carelessly on the bathroom floor. There was something terribly brazen—or innocent—about the girl.

"Oh, yes, a bath," Ruiz whispered. He reached into the box and stroked the bottom of her thigh with his finger. "Lovely, no?"

Lagarde was offended. It was ridiculous, he knew, but he felt a kind of jealousy overwhelm him. He repressed an urge to insult the little man.

Turning to Gruen, he asked, "Will you be here on the thirty-first?"

"Where else would I be?"

"I have to go. I'm late," Lagarde said, still flustered by his emotions.

"I'll see you then, yes?" The old man followed him with small steps out into the hall.

"We'll see," the attorney said as he hurried toward the elevators. "Maybe."

LAUREN SLEPT WITH Lagarde for the first time a week before Christmas. Two days of depositions from crewmen of the beached barge and its tug had been scheduled at Daigle, Johnson, and she had arranged to spend the intervening Thursday night in New Orleans. Finishing their work about eight, the two attorneys treated themselves to an expensive dinner in the French Quarter. They laughed easily with each other, and by the time one of them looked at a watch it was well past eleven. Lagarde offered to walk his colleague back to her hotel on Canal Street. She took his arm, and they huddled together against the cold wind that shook the shop signs of the Quarter. In the lobby of the hotel, Lauren kissed him on the cheek. He smiled as he waved good-bye from the revolving doors.

By the time they had concluded the last deposition late Friday afternoon, Lauren had already called her roommate in Baton Rouge to say she would not be home that night. In fact, she did not see her roommate again until Sunday evening, when, giddy and exhausted, she announced that she was in love.

For Lagarde, the weekend had disturbed and then simplified everything. The furtive glances across the conference table Friday morning, his clumsy invitation at lunch to stay through the weekend, the shy and tender smile with which she accepted, the interminable afternoon of lawyerly questions and answers, the confusion about what to do with her car at the hotel—everything, all the complexities and awkwardness and impatience of sudden love, fell with their clothes to the floor when at last, after dinner and a few fortifying drinks, the young couple shut the door of Lagarde's house behind them and put out the lights.

The next Thursday, Christmas Eve, the attorney slipped away early from the firm's holiday party to meet Lauren in Baton Rouge for dinner and to exchange gifts. Before he left, though, Tommy Hinton pulled him aside. "Listen, I got the report back from our appraiser this morning," his friend whispered conspiratorially over a half-empty glass of bourbon. "That statue, you know, for your daddy, it checked out. And it's worth at least 175, maybe 200,000. A hell of a deal." Clapping his friend on the back for the favor, Lagarde realized that he had almost forgotten about the sculpture during the last few days.

The following morning, snuggling beneath a comforter that had belonged to the girl's grandmother, the two lovers kissed and teased. Lauren wanted him to join her family for Christmas dinner that afternoon, but he had promised to celebrate the holiday with Nana at the hotel where she lived in New Orleans. "Well," said the young woman, struggling into her nightgown beneath the covers, "at least we can have a Christmas breakfast together."

By the time Lagarde had dressed, Lauren's roommate and her boyfriend had emerged from their room and were stumbling around the kitchen, begging for coffee. They had come in late, and so Lagarde had not yet met them. Stephanie, a friend from Lauren's undergraduate days at LSU, was a medical technician; her fiancé, Vic, was an intern at Our Lady of the Lake Hospital. The four shared a quiet breakfast. While Stephanie and Vic stared off into the flowering vines and blue lattice of the kitchen wallpaper, Lauren slipped her hand into Lagarde's beneath the table.

☙

NANA WAS WAITING in the lobby of the Wharton when her grandson arrived. "I would've come up and gotten you," Lagarde said, embracing the old woman gently.

"No, the reservations were for 12:30. I didn't want them to give our table away."

"Nana, it's just 12:30 now."

"Good, then we can go right in." She took her grandson's arm.

Seated near the small fountain at the rear of the dining room, Lagarde was pleased to be spending Christmas with his grandmother. With his parents' move to New York and the death of his aunt last year, he was the last of Nana's family still in the city. Sooner or later, his father would insist on bringing the old woman north to live with them. But for another year or two, she could manage on her own—with Lagarde's occasional help. Indulging finally in champagne and the restaurant's famously excessive desserts, grandmother and grandson enjoyed a merry afternoon, with the conversation somehow always returning to Lagarde's new friend in Baton Rouge. The young man insisted on paying for the meal, and Nana invited him up to her rooms for coffee.

As an ancient bellhop brought them to the top floor of the hotel in the small elevator, Lagarde's grandmother whispered discreetly how pleased she was that he had found a young lady. "It's about time," she said.

Lagarde protested that they had just met and who could say what would come of it.

Nana gave him one of the smirks he remembered from childhood. "Who are you trying to fool? You're going to marry this girl."

They had reached her floor. As the old woman stepped out into the hall, Lagarde stayed in the elevator. *She's right,* he thought to himself with a start.

The bellman turned to his passenger. "Top floor," he wheezed. "Going down."

Lagarde followed his grandmother to her door. The furniture from the big house on Prytania looked odd squeezed into the apartment. Nana had moved here a few years after the death of Lagarde's grandfather. Four or five other elderly New Orleanians kept apartments at the Wharton; it was an old tradition that only a few hotels in town still honored. She picked up the phone and ordered coffee from room service.

Lagarde had managed to avoid the subject of the sculpture, but as they waited for the coffee to be delivered, he offhandedly mentioned the Degas he had been offered. Nana, enamored of the French, recalled her honeymoon in Paris.

"Your grandfather never had a taste for it, but he bought me my little Renoir pastel as a wedding present. It was our last day before coming home. The weather was terrible, but we were walking on the Rue Rivoli when I saw it through a window. I dragged him into the shop. Oh, it made me weak, I loved it so much. But he said no, absolutely not. I was furious with him—what a spoiled young thing I was. Then, that night, when we got back from dinner, there was the little drawing propped against the pillow of our bed. He was such a stinker, your grandfather."

Lagarde tried to change the subject. The last thing he wanted was to trade on his grandmother's happy memories. But Nana refused to talk about anything else. She demanded all the details. She even dragged from him the financial arrangements he might make.

"So you need a loan of $125,000 by next week," the old lady said, nodding her head, "but you'll pay back $100,000 as soon as you sell the house."

"And the car and the stocks," Lagarde added, with growing anxiety.

"Why not?" Nana smiled mischievously. "Why not?"

Lagarde felt his heart beating too quickly in his chest.

"And I'll tell you what," his grandmother continued, "if you marry Lauren, the other $25,000 will be my wedding present to you." Then wagging her finger at him, she said laughing, "But if you don't get married, you'll have to pay back every penny." She instructed him to call Deacon Gilbert, the family's attorney, on Monday afternoon. "Deek'll make the arrangements," she promised.

After they had had their coffee, Nana took Lagarde into her bedroom to show him the Renoir. He had not seen it since he was a child. It left him, as it had his grandfather, absolutely cold. The pretty young girl, smudged in pink and purple and blue, touched nothing within him, but his grandmother, standing next to him, brushed tears from her cheeks with a pale, wrinkled hand.

❦

HE HAD JUST gotten home from Nana's when there was a knock at the door. He peeked out through the living room window. "Surprise," Lauren shouted from the porch.

Once inside, she explained that she had gotten back to her apartment after lunch with her family and couldn't think of anything to do except to work on an admiralty case she was handling that involved a barge and a sandbar. So she had popped down to New Orleans to see if her cocounsel might want to spend the weekend collaborating with her on some legal research.

"Oh, I see. You want to get into my briefs, huh? Well, come on then," Lagarde agreed, pushing her into the bedroom, "we'd better get to work."

As the evening progressed to several courses of Chinese food, an old movie on cable, and finally a few hours of intermittent sleep in each other's arms on the sofa, their playfulness yielded to passion.

Lagarde woke to the rush of water. Wrapping himself in a blanket, he pushed open the bathroom door. Lauren, reclining in the huge, old tub with ball-and-talon legs, instinctively tried to cover her nakedness. Then she smiled at herself and shyly let her hands slip back into the water.

Dropping the blanket around his feet, Lagarde joined her in the tub. The water rushed up to her throat as he sat down across from her. She tried to lift her long hair out of the water; it lay along her shoulder like wet, dark silk.

"Give me your foot," he said.

She slid her foot along the porcelain until it slipped into the stirrup of his hand. Lifting it up on to his stomach, he cupped the top of it with his other hand and massaged it till she closed her eyes and sighed.

As HIS GRANDMOTHER had promised, her attorney had the check waiting for him when he called Monday afternoon. Deek knew better than to ask what the money was for. "Can you pick it up tomorrow?" the old lawyer wondered. "I was just leaving for the club."

So after lunch on Tuesday, Lagarde returned to work with a check for $125,000 in his pocket. He was most afraid that someone in the office might see it; such a check would be difficult to explain, particularly if he tried to tell the truth about it.

He drove around for a long time before going home that night. In fact, he even took a ride out to Lake Pontchartrain. He knew he was approaching the moment when he would have to make a decision. He had only two days left.

A 5 P.M. filing deadline for a motion in a wrongful death suit brought by the widow of an oil rig worker occupied the attorney's attention for most of the next day. By the time a messenger had hurried off with the motion, Lagarde was almost relieved to discover that it was too late to make it over to Gruen's.

That night, he had trouble sleeping. He would make up his mind to buy or not to buy the sculpture; then, almost asleep, he would have second thoughts and roll onto his back to rethink the whole decision. As he grumpily ordered coffee and a blueberry muffin at the breakfast shop in his office building on New Year's Eve, Lagarde made up his mind for the last time.

He called Gruen at ten o'clock and arranged to pick up *The Tub* at the end of the day. Having committed himself to the purchase, he grew more and more excited as the morning matured into afternoon and the afternoon steeped into early evening. By four, most of the partners had already left for the long weekend. A few minutes after the hour, Lagarde pulled out of the parking lot and fought the early traffic to the Effinger Building. Finally finding a space, he dumped a handful of change in the meter and hurried into the building.

Gruen, already in his worn overcoat, was waiting. Somehow, he had dragged the unwieldy crate into the front room. His daughter, he explained, was picking him up downstairs in fifteen minutes. He handed over the authentication papers.

"Well," said Lagarde, taking a deep breath, "here's the check." Endorsing it with his Montblanc, he presented the old man with the slip of paper he had carried in his wallet for the last two days.

"But the tax," stammered Gruen. "Where's the tax?"

"I thought it was included."

"Included? Do you think I could sell you a Degas for $115,000? Even a maquette?" The old man leaned against the crate.

"It's all I've got." Lagarde realized in a kind of terror that he was in danger of losing her, but he bluffed anyway. "If it's not enough, I'll understand." He held out his hand to take back the check.

The old man folded the check and put it in his shirt pocket. "You're robbing me," he complained.

Lagarde had seen this before in negotiations for settlements. He sensed that even without the tax, the dealer was still making a comfortable profit. The lawyer wondered how cheaply the old man had gotten the piece in the first place.

Now that he had the money, Gruen was impatient to close up. Still grumbling, he locked the door behind him as Lagarde struggled down the hall with the crate. He held the elevator for the young man, who carefully placed the container onto the carpeted floor as they made their slow descent. Gruen said nothing, and when the elevator doors opened on the first floor, he hurried off without even a good-bye.

Lagarde muscled the crate into the trunk of his car but had to use a rope to tie it shut. Driving home, he avoided as many bumps as he could, afraid he would find the sculpture cracked in half when he pulled into his driveway.

It seemed to take forever to get home, but once he did struggle through the door with the heavy container, he felt a secret joy begin to seep through him. He gently lowered his burden onto the floor. Unlatching the top and stooping over the statue, he felt the weight of it along his spine as he began to lift. He stopped and bent his knees. As the bottom of the statue cleared the edge of the box, he quickly set the sculpture down on a kilim he had gotten at auction. Lagarde hadn't considered where he might put the piece. He had very little furniture, though what he had was of value, antiques carefully collected in the dusty warehouses of the city's oldest dealers.

Surveying the room, he chose as the statue's pedestal the nineteenth-century gaming table he had found the year before at an estate sale. He covered the polished mahogany with a tablecloth and thick towels. Then he lifted the sculpture onto its center. He pulled the sturdy cockfighting chairs, upholstered in green leather, away from the table and adjusted the dimmer on the little chandelier. In the shimmering light of the crystal lamp, he admired *The Tub*.

Now that the work was his, he examined it more closely. He was shocked to discover the lips of a vulva pinched between her fleshy thighs and curls of thick hair scored across her pubes. But these were secrets, hidden by the bronze patina of the wax and the shadows of her raised legs.

For the first time, he touched the body of the bather. It looked so much like bronze, his fingers were surprised that the breast was not cool. The hardened wax of the figure felt like flesh grown suddenly taut under an unexpected hand.

Lagarde opened a small cabinet and withdrew a bottle of brandy. Pouring himself a snifter, he sat across the room admiring his sculpture. But in the midst of his pleasure, he began, inexplicably, to sadden.

Even after he had gone to his bedroom to dress for the evening, he could not shake the melancholy that had tainted his happiness. In fact, as he buttoned the leather thongs of his braces to the black, satin-striped pants and as he fumbled with the unfamiliar knot of a silk bow tie, his mood worsened, like the storm whipping out of the Gulf and across the marshes.

A COLD RAIN lashed his windshield by the time he reached the interstate. Having promised Lauren that he would be in Baton Rouge by nine o'clock, he had to drive faster than he would have liked in such nasty weather. Her parents were hosting their annual New Year's Eve party, and she was eager for them to meet her new friend. Though he had hinted at his misgivings about being introduced to them at a party, Lauren was confident her mother and father would love him as much as she did. He almost hadn't noticed her use of "love." It was the first time either one of them had said the word. To his surprise, it left him not—as he would have expected—peevish, but rather calm, almost placid, as if it were the right word, after all, to describe the pleasure he felt in her company. It might have slipped by unnoticed in the distraction of his concern about meeting her parents if Lagarde hadn't caught Lauren's slight pause and sidelong glance as she said it.

He repeated her sentence as his car skimmed over the slick concrete of the highway.

"BUT WHY DO YOU have to leave so early?" Lauren asked groggily. Then, sitting up in the bed and brushing the sleep from her eyes, she realized, "It's still dark outside."

As he gathered up his cummerbund and bow tie from the floor and stuffed them into a pocket of his dinner jacket, Lagarde explained that he had to go.

"I thought we were going to spend the weekend together," Lauren said, the hurt creeping into her voice. "Didn't you have a good time last night?"

Lagarde sat down beside her on the bed. "I had a wonderful time."

"Were my parents awful?"

"I love your parents," he said, then added after a pause, "and I love you."

Lauren strained in the darkness to see his eyes.

He bent and kissed her. "But I have to go," he whispered.

"At least let me make you breakfast."

He relented. "Just coffee."

They did not say much as they sipped from steaming mugs beneath the harsh kitchen light. Lagarde tried to find a way to explain why he had to return to New Orleans immediately, but with only a few hours sleep and still a bit dazed from the New Year's Eve festivities, he couldn't think how to make Lauren understand his anxiety about his statue.

In fact, he hadn't yet told her anything about the Degas. When he considered what he had done—spending $125,000 on a work of art—and even more when he considered what remained to be done—selling his house, his car, and his stocks to pay back his grandmother's loan—he began to see how foolhardy it would all appear to the woman whom, yes, he loved.

"I could come with you," she suddenly said, interrupting his thoughts. "We can call my mother from New Orleans and tell her we can't come to dinner. She won't mind; they're having a whole house of friends over to see LSU in the Cotton Bowl. It's just going to be a buffet."

"No, I wouldn't take you away from your family on a holiday," Lagarde protested. "Why don't you come tomorrow?"

"I can't. We have the firm's touch football game tomorrow. I have to play. Remember? You were going to be my cheerleader. Anyway, what's so important in New Orleans on New Year's morning?"

"I can't tell you. It's a surprise."

As they stood at the door, Lauren gave Lagarde a small, pouting kiss. He wanted to explain, but instead he hurried down the steps and out to his car.

Driving back to the city as dawn began to stain the horizon, he had a long conversation with himself, trying to ferret out the diverse sources of his worry. The most obvious was practical: he might not have insurance on the piece. It hadn't occurred to him that he might need a rider on his policy to cover such an expensive addition to his household furnishings, but at 4:30 A.M., tossing restlessly in Lauren's bed, the thought had suddenly pierced him. A second arrow of anxiety followed the first. The sculpture was still sitting on his dining room table, unprotected and exposed. His neighborhood, though relatively safe, had witnessed its share of crime since he had moved in. The piece might already have been stolen; surely burglars realized many people were away from their homes on New Year's Eve. Or it might even have been vandalized by teenagers hopped up on booze and drugs. Lying awake in the dark, Lagarde had taken a deep breath and made himself admit that his fears were exaggerated. Still, his insurance agent wouldn't be in the office until Monday; he decided he had to stay with the statue until then.

But money wasn't the only source of concern. He had felt guilty in Lauren's arms. In part, he was troubled by keeping a secret from her; however, he was too embarrassed and too uncertain of her response to reveal his purchase. There was another barb of guilt, though, that he was less ready to acknowledge. Smothering Lauren in his kisses, he had felt somehow unfaithful to the woman in *The Tub*. It was ridiculous, he knew, and as soon as he realized what had been rasping his conscience, it ceased to trouble him. But now, driving through the damp pine forests west of New Orleans, he recognized that he was as much owned by the work of art as owner of it. He could not imagine it as less than a petulant mistress, lolling indifferently in her bath. It was no mere lump of wax, of plaster, of canvas. It was a small, exquisite woman with a claim on him.

Lost in thought, he nearly hit an armadillo, dead on the highway.

WHEN LAGARDE LEFT for work Monday morning, he hid the statue—replaced in its crate—among some empty boxes in the laundry room. Even once the insurance had been secured, Lagarde rarely removed the woman from her hiding place, particularly after his real estate agent began to show the house to prospective buyers.

It did not take long to sell the house, though the price was less than he had hoped. An antiques dealer made up the difference but left Lagarde with only a mattress, a chair or two, a small table. He waited until he had moved to his new apartment on the streetcar line before he sold his car. The stocks were worth a bit more than the last time he had checked, but with commissions and fees and all the unexpected costs of divesting oneself of material possessions, Lagarde found he still had to withdraw most of his $5,000 in savings to equal the $100,000 he owed his grandmother.

When he telephoned to let Nana know he'd sold his house, she dismissed his concerns about the money. "Just send the check to Deek after the closing," she said, making clear her indifference about the matter. But she was insistent on one point. "When am I going to get to see this beautiful woman of yours?"

"Well, I've got her in a crate right now," Lagarde said, trying to put his grandmother off.

"In a crate?" Nana repeated, horrified. "The poor girl. You should be ashamed."

Lagarde suddenly realized what his grandmother was talking about. "Oh, you mean Lauren."

"Of course I mean Lauren. You're not seeing someone else, are you?"

"No, no," Lagarde protested, "I thought you wanted to see the sculpture, the woman by Degas that I bought."

"Yes, her, too," the old lady said, still a bit disconcerted.

"I promise, as soon as I've got my new apartment all straight, you'll come for dinner. You can meet both women at the same time."

Nana laughed lightly. "So what did Lauren say when she found out you'd sold everything to buy a work of art?"

Lagarde coughed. "I haven't told her yet. I want it to be a surprise."

There was a silence on the other end of the line. Finally, the old woman said, "It's none of my business, of course, Peter. And I think it's utterly charming what you've done. And daring. But . . ."

"Yes," he said resignedly, "you're right."

HE HAD JOKED to himself that he might have to marry Lauren just to avoid paying back the other $25,000 Nana had given him, but he began to wonder whether Lauren would have him after weeks of inexplicable behavior. She had sympathetically accepted one excuse after another. He was tired of worrying about a house; he preferred an apartment. His antique furniture was oppressive. He wanted a less cluttered, more minimalist look. The car was too much trouble, too ostentatious, and he insisted that the weekend trips to Baton Rouge he now made on the bus were preferable to driving—they gave him a chance to catch up on his reading. But when at last he allowed Lauren to see his bare new apartment, she betrayed her misgivings.

Standing in the doorway, she looked for something to admire in Lagarde's new place. Two wooden chairs faced each other across the gray carpet of an otherwise empty living room. There was nothing upon which to place the crystal vase she had brought as a housewarming present. She handed the wrapped package awkwardly behind her to Lagarde, who still stood in the hall.

"Let me show you the rest," he said without much confidence.

The gray carpet lapped at the white floor tiles of a tiny kitchen. A counter jutting out past the far wall of cabinets concealed a windowless dining alcove. There, a small black table plunged its stubby legs into another swatch of gray carpet.

Beyond lay the bath and bedroom, where a mattress sprawled on the floor. The phone rested on a book beside the simple bed.

Still holding the gift, he sighed. Lauren took his hand, and she made him sit with her on the edge of the mattress.

"I just want to tell you," she said, taking a deep breath, "that I've managed to save some money over the last two years. If you're having trouble right now, I want you to have it. It's not much—"

Lagarde interrupted her. "Thank you," he said.

"No matter how it happened—gambling, or whatever. It's yours, all of it."

Lagarde shook his head. "No, that's not it," he began. "I have to show you something." He stood up. "I want you to wait in here until I call you. OK?"

He closed the bedroom door behind him and unlocked the large hall closet, on which he had had a dead bolt installed before he moved in.

When Lauren emerged from the bedroom, Lagarde had extinguished all the lights except for three track lamps in the breakfast nook. In dimmed incandescence on the black table rested the sculpture. The shafts of muted light fell upon the wax face, a breast, and the legs of the nude woman. Slight shadows gave weight to her small body.

Lauren walked silently around the statue, once pausing to shyly touch the hand of the figure. Coming round to where she had started, she looked to Lagarde for an explanation.

"It's a Degas. It cost me everything." He couldn't bring himself to excuse it as an investment. "I just thought . . ." He stopped and sighed.

"She's exquisite," Lauren said. Her voice trembled as if she had been wounded in some way. "But you gave up everything for her."

Lagarde understood, all at once, that he was about to lose her. Without warning, he took Lauren in his arms, kissing her hard and unyieldingly as she tried to break free of him. He pressed her against the wall and slipped a hand inside her blouse. Then she was unbuckling his pants, pulling his shirt up. They fell to the floor and entwined beneath the indifferent gaze of the brazen nude woman.

Hours later, exhausted and bruised, the couple slept on the mattress in the back room. Just before dawn, Lagarde rolled awake from restless sleep and walked to the kitchen for water.

The dimmed lights still illuminated the statue. Naked, he stood before the work of art, his weariness swelling into fury over the sacrifices required of him by the woman in the tub, forever bathing, forever demanding his attention.

He began to see the folly of his devotion. For a moment, he could have done anything; he could have smashed the mocking face, the teasing body. But he was already too ridiculous, and he could not bring himself to hurt the beautiful creature.

He fled into the bedroom. The fringes of light from the other room cast themselves over Lauren, who had twisted free of the covers. The hair curling like cloth against the face, a breast cupped in her hand, the legs bent to expose the dark frills of her genitalia, a long arm dangling over the edge of the mattress onto the floor—Lagarde recognized, with a slight shudder, who lay asleep at his feet.

He wavered. "So this is love," he said, hopelessly, then knelt among the sheets frothing about her ankles and touched her.

Gregory's Fate

It was in late adolescence that my childhood friend Gregory first gave evidence of the unique talent that would doom him to the most pathetic of fates.

A shy and self-conscious young man, Greg must have discovered the earliest manifestations of his strange gift in the privacy of his room or, perhaps, in the steaming waters of his tub. I am sure that these signs—what we would later call "symptoms"—were so slight as to barely attract his attention. There may have been a certain slackness to his thigh, an inexplicably enlarged knuckle, a pattern of bright pigments emerging on the pale skin stretched across his breastbone, but nothing so extraordinary as to frighten him into the waiting room of a physician. Too, whatever happened to trouble his drowsing bath or daydreaming solitude would have waned in a few hours, leaving him unsure that he had really seen anything at all in the dresser mirror or beneath the cloudy water.

Eventually, curiosity and vague anxiety would have impelled Gregory to rub the erupting pores or poke the knob of bone protruding on the back of his hand. He would have been startled to see his manipulations affect the physical changes he was witnessing. Mesmerized as he watched himself attenuate his arm into a wing and twist his toes into talons, Gregory would not have noticed his fear yield to wonder. Hours later, turning his feathered face to the mirror, how he must have marveled at his miraculous transformation.

The change was not, as in literature or even as in film, instantaneous. Flesh and bone had to be worked into fresh relationships. Each piece had to be tooled. The latent memory of each ligament and tendon had to be massaged into oblivion. Then each aching new joint had to be rotated into each raw new socket. Bones had to be bent, the skull deformed, the skin hardened. It could take hours.

Once, after he had revealed to me his secret, I walked in on my friend in the process of changing into a dog. He seemed horribly disfigured and turned to me with the most pitiful and suppliant gaze I had ever encountered. I put my arms around his furry nape as he convulsed with the changes that wracked his body.

At the time, I thought it mere impulse that Greg had divulged the marvel of his transformations to me. But looking back, I see now that he intended to confess everything. Unwilling to confide in his parents, he really had no one else but me with whom to share his secret. Surely the urge to tell someone of the incredible things that were happening to his body must have nearly equaled the overwhelming urge to continue the strange experiments he was performing on himself.

At the same time, I sensed that his astounding gift was a source of shame for him. Gregory thought of his ability as simply a bad habit—one that he ought to overcome. He associated it, somehow, with his virginity. He confided to me his certainty that only a woman could cure him of the malleability that so afflicted his flesh and bones.

On the other hand, Greg lacked the malleability of imagination that might have allowed him to become what he appeared. No matter how extreme the transformation, he remained Gregory, a man, stuffed into a sack stitched in feathers or stretched over the long skeleton of a giraffe.

As summer progressed into the darker nights of autumn, the consequences of his adventures became increasingly worrisome. They were exactly the results anyone might engender by walking down the street in a gorilla costume. One might try to explain that it was just a joke, but to the terrified child whom the gorilla was attempting to calm, only a mumbled growl would seem to issue from the fierce, hairy mask. There was an enormous sense of the ridiculous surrounding these episodes—and a growing danger.

Regaining his original form took longer and longer. The flesh lacked its former resiliency. It sagged where it had been distended. It chafed where it had turned to scales. It erupted into boils where horns had sprouted.

Now the transformations lingered, at least in isolated patches on his body, beyond the weekends. For some days afterward, feathers would rustle beneath the wool of his slacks whenever he crossed his legs, or the ridges of a serrated spine would spoil the line of his blazer.

Gregory began to refer to the restoration of his true form as recuperation. "I'm still healing from the last attack," he confessed to me one Friday over the phone. I was no doctor, but I fell into the same terminology. I found myself calling Greg's unique talent a "condition." But neither of us could imagine what therapy or surgery might alleviate his disease.

It was in these low days of worry and suffering that Gregory first pointed out Esperanza to me. We were in a café on Royal Street, sharing a newspaper and sipping coffee after classes at the university, when a tiny young woman, encumbered by swollen shopping bags and immense packages, lumbered through the narrow carriageway to the patio where we sat. Disgorging her purchases onto a table next to ours, she collapsed into an ancient wrought iron chair. The bags, I noticed, were emblazoned with the crests of the most expensive boutiques in the French Quarter and the huge packages were bound in the delicate ribbons of the city's most exclusive shops. Taking a quarter from her change purse, she tapped on the edge of her table till a waiter scurried over to take her order.

Greg seemed to take no notice of the hubbub. Slowly turning the pages of the *Times-Picayune,* he was engrossed, it appeared, in the small type of the stock exchange reports. It should have occurred to me that, having never played the market, my friend had no reason to peruse the financial section. In fact, the newspaper was merely a blind behind which Gregory savored the good fortune of our chance encounter with the woman he adored.

Though he had never met her, Gregory had somehow ferreted out her name and her family's history from those mutual acquaintances that so complicate life in a small city. Esperanza Obliga was the youngest of four daughters of a wealthy Nicaraguan family who had escaped their country after the Sandinista rebellion. Though reduced in circumstances, the family survived on their vast holdings in Brazil and in the Yucatan as well as on their accounts in Switzerland and Miami. Señor Obliga had been an intimate of the recently assassinated dictator, Anastasio Somoza, and therefore kept a low profile in the émigré community. "Despite her father's position in the government, Esperanza's heart, of course, was with the revolutionaries who over- threw the detested tyrant," Gregory assured me, though how he might have glimpsed the workings of her heart—having never so much as spoken to her—was beyond my powers of comprehension.

Personally, once we did meet her, I found Señorita Obliga a rather odd girl, with her annoying habit of lapsing into trances in the middle of conversations. Gregory furiously defended her: "What do you expect, Francis, when you insist upon such tedious arguments? Even I find them a bit boring." Her pinched face with its huge black eyes and her small, tubercular frame reminded me, I suppose, of an albino bat. But Gregory worshiped her.

The slightest departure from the indifference with which Esper- anza usually responded to my friend's embarrassing flattery would thrill him for days. Her smallest patronizing gesture of gratitude for the costly presents he laid at her feet would send him back to the stores on another shopping spree that left him yet more deeply in debt. At last, though, even the love-besotted eyes of poor Greg began to see that Esperanza's tiny heart remained closed to him.

In a desperate final bid for her tenderness, he determined to employ the full resources of his metamorphic powers. He imagined over emptied mugs of beer—in which he more and more indulged—how he might dazzle the object of his affection with his transformations, and thus woo her.

I counseled my friend to find another way. If his desire insisted upon Esperanza Obliga, then he should write poems to her, join her church, go to work for her father. Over the last months, the transformations had grown steadily more debilitating; I worried about the medical consequences if Greg, in his fevered state of mind, should undertake a program of these dangerous changes.

Gregory took my advice—in part. When I next saw him, he clutched the catechism of the Obligas' church. Not only was he preparing for baptism, but he proudly announced that a friend of his family had secured a part-time position for him as personal secretary to Esperanza's father. Unfortunately, though, Gregory had no talent for poetry. He was grateful for my advice, but he remained convinced that only his special gift could reveal to the woman he loved the depth of his affection. When I tried to remind him of the dangers, he grew testy with me.

Seeing that it was pointless to continue my efforts at dissuasion, I agreed to assist my friend in the elaborate sequence of transformations he had planned. (I thought, if something went wrong, at least I could get him to a hospital.) To assuage my concern, he assured me that once he had completed the first metamorphosis, his body would yield easily to the others. "It's just getting back to being human that's difficult," he admitted.

Gregory had prepared a script for me. I was to serve as a kind of narrator for Esperanza as my friend metamorphosed from eagle to gazelle to dolphin to pony and then back to Gregory. He had penned a rather awkward introduction and series of interludes in which he suggested, employing the hoariest of clichés, the relationship of these creatures to the emotions he felt for the young lady. "My heart soars like an eagle," he had written, "whenever I see you." A literature major at the university, I offered to revise his narrative, but Gregory declined. He trusted Esperanza to see his love for what it truly was.

Though, of course, I did not say so, I was terribly concerned about Greg's wounded pride and broken heart when Esperanza, if she even agreed to attend the little performance, reacted to his ridiculous sideshow act—as I had no doubt she would—with the condescending laugh she seemed to reserve for him. I felt certain no good could come of revealing his secret to Señorita Obliga.

Gregory had chosen to start the performance as an eagle because it required the most preparation; in fact, he thought it might take him three or four hours. That afternoon I locked him in the small campus theater we had reserved from the drama department; I had overcome the objections of the departmental secretary by assuring her that we were rehearsing scenes to be performed in an English class on the theater of the Middle Ages. Then at seven o'clock, as Greg had previously arranged, I picked up Esperanza and drove her to the university. It was obvious from our conversation in the car that she had agreed to come only out of curiosity. Gregory had given her no hint as to what she might expect, but he promised her a spectacle that would remain unmatched in her lifetime. I assured her that he had not exaggerated.

Having shown Esperanza to the specific seat that Greg had chosen for her, I climbed the steps to the stage and peeked behind the mangy velvet curtain. Gregory, beautifully transformed into a magnificent bird, nested on the floor. I crossed to the edge of the stage, and standing on its apron where I could reach the curtain's draw lines, I took the script from my pocket and began to read aloud.

When I had reached the end of Gregory's cliché-ridden introduction, I hauled on the rope in my hand and parted the curtain. Waddling forward on claws that scrabbled along the wooden planks of the stage, the eagle squawked a contorted call into the darkened auditorium where Esperanza sat. I think the feathered throat was trying to say, "It's me—Gregory." But to be honest, it sounded more like the rasping caw of a crow. I squinted into the spotlights, which I had turned on before we began, trying to see Esperanza's reaction. I could barely make out her form in the silent hall. Dragging his wings behind him, Gregory retreated, and I closed the curtain.

A bit nervous, I read the next passage too quickly. The grace of the gazelle, to which Gregory alluded in the narration as an image of Esperanza's beauty, was absent from the hairy beast with twisted horns that pawed the stage when, a few minutes later, I parted the curtain for the second transformation. Obviously rushed in its creation, the animal seemed a crude approximation of so lithe a creature. Greg had needed more time; in fact, a few feathers still clung to his hindquarters.

I knew that the third transformation was the simplest, so I hurriedly closed the curtain on the crude gazelle and began to recite a homage to the idyllic life of the dolphin, a life of love beneath the waves. I must admit that I embroidered Gregory's prose with some of my own rhetorical inventions. Hearing my revisions, Greg interrupted me with a string of high-pitched barks. I drew open the curtain to reveal a pair of intelligent eyes regarding me above a silver snout. Dragging himself forward on his pectoral fins and slapping his flat tail against the stage, Gregory seemed on the verge of speaking, but the squeals that issued from his ridged jaws explained nothing. Once again, I closed the curtain.

Esperanza, infuriated at having wasted half an hour on such a ridiculous menagerie, made clear her utter lack of belief that these creatures could be manifestations of the awkward boy who plagued her with his incessant fawning.

Storming up the aisle, Esperanza interrupted my speech about the relationship of horses to love. Pushing past my feeble efforts to stop her, she tore open the curtain. Over her scrawny shoulder, I saw Gregory trying to cover his nakedness with his still-webbed hands. Pitiful under the harsh light of the single bulb that illuminated the backstage, he recklessly tugged upon his arms and legs, grasped his jaw in both hands to elongate his chin, flicked the top of his ears into points. Before the amazed and dumbstruck Esperanza, Gregory completed his performance, finally turning his long, sleek neck to the tiny girl and licking her outstretched palm.

Clapping her hands and giggling furiously, Esperanza leapt upon the dappled back of the little pony and, driving her heels into its haunches, whipped it round the bare stage with her belt. The pathetic whinnying at each lash punctuated the clopping of its unshod hooves against the worn wooden flooring.

A month later, the young couple was married in one of the most extravagant ceremonies the city had ever witnessed. That evening, while the reception roared on in the ballroom below, the new Mr. and Mrs. Gregory Kunstler ascended in an ornate elevator, whose carpet had been littered with red rose petals, to the bridal suite atop the hotel.

And what became of Gregory, my friend? He prays in Esperanza's church, which forbids divorce. He works for his father-in-law, shamefully funneling arms and money to right-wing regimes in Central America. And late into the night, his wife makes him sit on the bathroom floor, where she pulls his fingers and rubs his flesh raw in the vain hope of reawakening the marvelous talent that disappeared—as Gregory had once guessed that it might—in her bony arms on their wedding night.

The Open Curtain

PIERCE SHOULD HAVE BEEN unsurprised, when he pulled up in front of his house at the end of a grueling three-day sales trip to the major clients in his new territory, that his wife had not yet drawn the dining room drapes. After all, just a few weeks before, sitting at dinner, even as late as dessert, nibbling the last of the season's berries, they and their children had still been able to look out across the evening lawn that swept down to the slowly darkening street. In fact, only as Caitlin and Tack cleared the table, each complaining incessantly about the other to their mother in the kitchen, did his own reflection, coalescing at last in the finally blackened panes, prompt Pierce to close the curtains before he settled himself in front of the television in the next room for the rest of the night.

But this evening, with darkness falling earlier as October withered into November, the huge bay window framed Charlotte setting each place for dinner, the whole scene illuminated by the small crystal chandelier floating above the table. Pierce watched her as she lifted a glass, turned it in her hand against the light, and replaced it above a plate. He was touched when she laid out a fourth place setting, even though he had warned her Wednesday morning that he might not be home until well after dinner on Friday.

She drifted back and forth in the window, and he realized he was craning his neck around the headrest of the passenger seat to keep her in view. He smiled at himself and was about to get out of the car—he had already leaned over to the glove compartment to press the trunk release—when Caitlin stormed into the dining room, tears streaming down her cheeks. Expecting to see her mother hurry to comfort her, Pierce grew uneasy as the forlorn girl sobbed alone in the room, which seemed to him, for the first time, ridiculously ornate. Finally, her mother appeared, on the other side of the table, and angrily waved a fork at the teenager.

He continued to watch, transfixed by the drama enacted in the brightly lit room. Caitlin turned her back on Charlotte and stared out the window, the dark glass no doubt returning her petulant glare. Behind her, the older woman continued to rage, circling the table and spinning the girl around by her shoulders. Suddenly, Caitlin's head jerked sideways. It took Pierce a moment to realize Charlotte had slapped her child.

He felt his body slump in the Lincoln's leather seat, as if he were the one who had been struck. I should go in, he told himself.

But now they were hugging each other, mother and daughter, both in tears. Her arm around Caitlin, Charlotte walked the girl toward the kitchen.

Pierce sat very still, stunned by what he had witnessed. He had always assumed that Charlotte, like himself, had never raised a hand to the children. What kind of mother, he pondered, hits her daughter? Certainly not the mother of his children—or so he had believed. Shaken, he could not go in, not yet, and it was clear that neither had been able to see him in the dark. So he waited, intently watching the window for the next scene.

By the time they returned, Tack had joined them. Charlotte played with Caitlin's hair, pushing it back over the girl's ears. Each seemed completely at ease with the other, affectionate in the way they touched, tender in their glances toward each other. The slap, somehow, had snapped the two back into balance.

Tack ignored them, moodily playing with his food as Charlotte heaped it upon his plate. The boy's face was older than Pierce had noticed before. Already the chiseled planes of a man's cheeks had hardened beneath what looked from a distance like very cruel eyes. He was indifferent, it was obvious, to the other two at the table, though both seemed willing to pamper his pouting.

Pierce watched his family for another few minutes, disturbed by how strange they seemed to him, how little he recognized in them when he looked closely. He began to study wife, daughter, son.

The bay window was crosshatched into a grid of small rectangles. He focused on one pane at a time, examining each frame for something he had always missed, something he had never noticed. Almost immediately, he saw a gesture he could not remember, one he must have somehow overlooked in the past, a hand moving in a slow arc. He followed the fingers to his daughter's mouth. In another pane, on the sideboard, a crystal pitcher he did not recognize trapped the light in its etched facets. It seemed that if only he could look hard enough, each frame would reveal a surprise—some invisible detail, some unconscious habit of the life lived in this house.

Finally, he was overcome by the same cloying guilt that eventually compels the reader of another's diary to shut the book. But he found he could not go in. The thought of joining the tableau he had secretly observed struck him as absurd as a member of an audience suddenly mounting the stage and assuming a role. So he sat discomforted in the car, waiting until the little family had finished its meal, cleared the table, and dimmed the chandelier sufficiently to see—through the suddenly transparent window—a man slinging a garment bag over his shoulder and hefting his case of samples and paperwork out of the deep trunk of the Lincoln Continental at their curb.

THOUGH TACK GREETED Pierce indifferently, his wife and his daughter were glad to have him home, Charlotte kissing her husband even as Caitlin gave her father a hug. Yet he almost felt swept up into someone else's life, mistaken for another man, for he could not escape the sense that the people in the house he had been watching were strangers.

When he had opened the front door, for example, bags still in hand, he was struck like a visitor by the cozy, musty smell of the home. The comfortable furniture, askew in the living room, now seemed to him worn and shoddy; the wallpaper, garish. Even the meal Charlotte had reheated for him tasted of odd spices, unfamiliar flavors.

He explained the peculiar sensation as simple weariness after three hard and unsuccessful days on the road. Despite all the rationales his manager had offered about the need to restructure Everfast's direct sales operations, everyone understood his new territory was a demotion. He told himself he was a victim of his own success, trapped between a market he had saturated with Everfast systems during his fifteen years at the firm and unrealistic annual growth targets determined by accountants of the Georgia conglomerate that had bought out the family-run company two years earlier. But there was more to it than that, he knew. He had suffered, even before the acquisition, a tailing-off of his accounts. If anything, the change in management had postponed the inevitable reckoning. But he had not taken advantage of his reprieve; remaining inattentive to the details of the job, he had been slow to service his accounts, restrained in touting upgrades and new product lines, unaggressive in soliciting clients. He had been coasting for years, but finally he had reached the bottom of the hill. And the new hill he had begun to climb on Wednesday was steeper than he had anticipated.

Perhaps, he conjectured, it was a kind of depression that had settled upon him, this distant watchfulness. Whatever its source, though, he could not avert his eyes from the revelations that presented themselves to him throughout the evening.

When Tack flung himself in front of the television, Pierce noticed the sixteen-year-old worry a gold bead in his left ear. When had that happened, the man wondered, and why hadn't they talked about it first? But he was too tired to fight about the earring and too shocked by the tattoo of black thorns—or were they teardrops?—that ringed his son's muscular arm just beneath the sleeve of a black T-shirt.

It was the boy's bare feet, though, that most deeply troubled the man. He still recalled the little footprint stamped on the hospital's certificate of live birth that Charlotte had mounted in Tack's baby book. But crossed upon each other on the living room carpet, these feet were large and powerful, a fully articulated musculature prepared for the young man who would rise above them. Pierce grasped, in their tense stretching and release, the metamorphosis already well under way behind the sneering lips and scornful eyes of his only son.

Caitlin, wary of her older brother, snuggled against her father on the sofa, still a little girl. He stroked her hair unconsciously, but finally looking at her face as she watched the TV, absorbed in a drama about parallel universes, he saw a cluster of faint scars he could not remember from childhood, a fleck of brown in her perfectly green eyes, a ridge thickening along her nose, and when she smiled, braces—how long had she been wearing braces? He wondered if he would have recognized her on the street, so different from the child he had imagined to be his daughter. How even would he have described her? There was nothing specific he could have said. And now that he thought of it, was she thirteen, or only twelve?

So the night unfolded, full of unnerving contradictions of stale memories by his new alertness to detail, until, exhausted, Pierce sprawled on the bedroom settee, sleepily fingering the raised, interlocking pattern of its satin upholstery. Charlotte undressed before him, inattentively casting off blouse and brassiere, indifferently dropping skirt and panties around her ankles, as if she were alone in the room.

Lounging on the little sofa, he was startled by her body, or not so much her body as its hundred forgotten secrets that seemed all at once to reveal themselves again to him, clambering like flowers in a crowded garden for his attention: the brown areola that puckered around each nipple, the thicket of fingers at the end of each hand, the lattice of disheveled hair around her face, the tangled vines of blue veins just beneath pale skin, the thatched tuft of red—no, he was astonished to realize finally, not red, but cinnamon, paprika—hairs wisping into tiny flames between her legs.

"Come here," he whispered.

Regarded so intently by her husband's gaze, Charlotte blushed, suddenly self-conscious, and covered her body with the blanket folded neatly at the foot of their bed. She smiled coquettishly to hide her embarrassment.

"Come here," he repeated, almost sternly.

It was a tone he had never used with her before, but she obeyed. Pierce reached up as she stood before him and uncoiled her two hands. The blanket fell away. He drew her down.

The naked woman huddled in his lap, loosening the tie still knotted at his throat, unbuttoning the shirt, working free the leather belt.

He kissed her neck and recognized the scent of—what?—coffee and something else, perhaps lemons. As he let her strip off his shirt, he nuzzled her belly and caught the faint, dusty smell of dry grain.

He touched the fretted furrow of her appendectomy scar, tested the palm of her hand with his thumb, traced her silhouette.

It was as if she were a woman he had never known before, as if he had never known any woman before. And he found more urgency in her slack flesh and aging eyes than in any erotic vision—those shadows of color floating across the television screen or puddling on the pages of a magazine—that he had ever enjoyed.

But who was she, this nude woman straining under him? No one he knew. Yet she called out, in a small voice, a name to which he answered.

As if unbound to her by affection or habit, he slowly explored this new body that writhed beneath him. Under his fresh fingers, clefts of flesh throbbed open, yielded, tensed shut. With the detachment of a connoisseur or an impostor, he watched himself make love to her until he was surfeited by the surprises of the evening and she lay limp beside him.

☙

HE HAD EXPECTED to wake, the next morning, like a man from a dream. As he drowsed beside Charlotte, who, well after midnight, still purred in the hollow of his shoulder, Pierce almost regretted that the strange evening must end, was already dissipating. He took for granted that a night of sleep would restore his old life, that his numb hand would reach for the clanging alarm in a few hours as it had for how many thousands of mornings, that he would rise only vaguely troubled by the perplexing dream he could not quite remember.

But he awoke to the appalling light, clotted in the lace filigree of the bedroom curtains, before the chiming clock could break the spell. The sleeping woman beside him, as if cringing from the dawn, hunched her bare back to the window. Stricken with misgivings, he leaned over her and cupped her face in his hand, lifting it gently from the pillow. The eye that opened on him, fluttered, then closed again in sleep was more gray than the blue he had thought to be the color of his wife's eyes. He lay the head down, unsettled.

Pierce dressed quickly, anxious to avoid his family. At the same time, though, he tried to honor his morning habits, as well as he could recall them, hoping by rote to find his way back to the life out of which he had somehow stepped. But again and again, he found himself stymied. When he reached for his razor in the medicine cabinet, his hand discovered an empty glass shelf; it took him a moment to remember he had not yet unpacked from his trip. When he stooped to tie his laces, he was unsure whether he usually crossed right over left or left over right. He had trouble with the half-Windsor knot he preferred for his tie, and he hesitated, on the way out, over the code to disarm the security system that monitored the house.

Pierce could not tell, as he sat in his car at the curb with the motor running, whether his life was unraveling or whether, perhaps, it was coiling more tightly—like the overwound spring of a watch—around nothing but itself.

Though the weekend, he still had a half day of work, the last remnant of old man Rittenberg's influence on the company. In fact, Pierce always looked forward to the slow Saturday mornings of glazed doughnuts and coffee, of anecdotes of the week's sales trips, of arguments about the teams playing that afternoon or the next. He parked in the factory lot, nearly deserted except for the big cars of the Everfast salesmen; the plant workers had traded their Saturday mornings for weekday split shifts under their union's new contract with Georgia Reditech.

As he walked among the still presses and fabricators toward the elevator to the fourth-floor offices, Pierce was jarred by the unfamiliar silence of the ominous machines. It was almost as if there were an echo to the silence in the vast room, a reverberating emptiness. The grimy windows of pebbled glass on the far wall filtered the harsh sunlight, casting pale, mottled shadows across the black machinery. He quickened his pace as he followed the aisle, banded in yellow safety perimeters, between die engravers, punch presses, and lathes.

Pierce watched the production floor fall away through the grates of the freight elevator as it rose. He stared, mesmerized, as the rows of green ceiling fixtures above the second-floor conveyor belts lowered themselves toward him till, in a blink of steel beams, they were reduced, just at eye level, to dust, clinging like downy hair to the wooden planks of the third floor. Already he could see above him, nestled in the roof's rafters, the loft of offices to which he ascended in the creaking elevator.

Lou Wallace, his sales manager, was waiting with a cup of coffee for Pierce. "Hey, buddy, so how'd it go?" Lou was all smiles, genial backslaps, and friendly winks. A nicer guy, Mr. Rittenberg always used to say, you wouldn't want to know.

Pierce wondered why he hadn't noticed it before, how old Lou had gotten in the last two years. "Great trip," he assured his manager, taking the coffee. "Nothing concrete, but a good start." He could see it had registered immediately: no orders, not one.

Lou was nodding, "Yeah, well, what more could we hope for? A good start, that's all we wanted." He nodded again, patting Pierce on the shoulder, then broke into a broad smile. "Hey, did you see? We got jelly doughnuts today—and a cake. It's Freddy's birthday."

The old man's disappointment about the trip could not have been plainer to Pierce. "I hope Inez doesn't hear you talking like that. I thought she had you on a diet."

Lou rubbed his stomach and feigned offense. "One doughnut, that's all." He didn't even wait for Pierce to smirk. "All right, two. But that's it." Turning to the other salesmen, he announced, "If my wife calls, I just had two doughnuts this morning—no, one. Right, Pierce?"

"That's right, Lou, one doughnut—and a half-dozen cheese Danishes."

As everyone laughed, Lou gave him a wink and moved on to Freddy's desk.

Pierce took a deep breath and settled into his chair. He felt guilty about letting Lou down, though until this morning he hadn't sensed his boss's anxiety. But now it was obvious, as the old man shuffled from one desk to another, joking with his sales force, nodding and smiling, that there was a problem.

Uneasy, Pierce refilled his cup behind the glass partition in the alcove. Looking through the framed window, stirring his coffee, he watched Freddy laughing, and Tom, and the others. They can't see it, the poor bastards, he thought, they just can't see. The laughter sounded far away, though everyone was right there in front of him.

⁂

WHEN PIERCE got home, a little after one, he found a note on the kitchen table: Charlotte had taken Caitlin for a haircut. Tack, he guessed, was still asleep.

He swung open the refrigerator door, looking for lunch.

Suddenly, he realized he didn't know how long he had been standing there—ten seconds, a minute—or why he had been memorizing
what he saw on the cold shelves. He closed the thick door and tried to
calm himself with a drink of water from the tap.

Swallowing slowly as he leaned over the empty sink, he noticed
beads of water splashed across the white porcelain, scattered like the
stones of a broken necklace.

He looked around the kitchen. Though he knew the history of
each piece that furnished the room—where they had purchased it,
who had marred its finish with a hot cup or dropped pot, even what
had been there before it—everything seemed to bristle with a fresh-
ness, an exactness, an immediacy that demanded his attention.

He reached over to the stove and twisted its black knobs; four blue
rings of fire sputtered into flame. He marveled at the extraordinary
sight and could barely bring himself to extinguish, one by one, the
flaming circles.

Pierce wandered through the house like a thief, lifting this orna-
ment or that, considering its value, listening for its heartbeat, returning it to the shelf. Every piece was as familiar as it was foreign to him,
and he felt as if he were lost in his own house or, perhaps, as if he had
been away for a very long time and finally had come home.

Yes, that was it, he decided. He had returned home after years of
detainment, though he was nagged by the knowledge that he had
been detained, all those years, in this very house.

Pierce wandered into his bedroom, into the bathroom, into
Caitlin's room. A kind of archaeologist in a newly excavated village,
he contemplated who could inhabit such a place, employ such arti-
facts, fashion such tools.

He was startled, opening yet another upstairs door, to discover a
body hanging over the edges of a small bed. He had forgotten Tack
might still be asleep.

The posters of heavy metal bands on the walls were interspersed
with vestiges of childhood, clumsily painted model airplanes hanging
by threads from the ceiling, an elementary school science project still

balanced atop a bookcase. Pierce picked up a notebook; it was filled with poems.

The face on the pillow was a surprise, too, so much younger asleep than awake.

As Pierce stood over Tack's bed, the boy's eyes opened. "What's wrong?" his son mumbled groggily.

"Nothing. Go back to sleep."

Tack started to rouse. "What are you doing in here?"

"I was looking for something."

"My things are private," the boy snarled, the anger pressing him awake.

"I wasn't looking through your things."

He could see that Tack was waiting for him to leave. Instead, he sat on the desk by the window.

"What are you so pissed about?"

"What?" The boy was taken off guard. He had never heard his father use that kind of language in the house.

"And why are you such a prick to your sister?"

He stammered, unsure how to respond.

"Get dressed," Pierce told him. "We're going out."

"I got plans," Tack protested.

"The hell with your plans."

Furious, the boy descended the stairs a few minutes later, wearing a long earring and a studded belt. His black boots were unlaced and flopped as he walked.

"Let's go," his father insisted, ignoring his complaints.

"Where are we going?"

"Breakfast."

"I don't eat breakfast."

"Get in the car."

Tack kept grumbling but did as he had been told. Pulling away from the curb, Pierce said to his son, "I didn't know you wrote poetry."

The boy was upset. "It's private."

"I didn't read any of it."

The car was close with silence.

Pierce knew what he should say next. "But I'd like to."

Tack was looking out his window at the thinning elms that slid past, one after another. Without turning back to his father, he said quietly, "There are a few you could see."

By the time father and son walked through the kitchen door an hour later, they were both laughing.

Charlotte and Caitlin, sharing a sandwich, looked at each other. It had been a long time since they had heard Tack's laugh.

"And don't forget those poems," Pierce called after the boy as he returned to his room.

"What poems?" Charlotte asked.

"Tack has been writing poetry."

"Really?" Caitlin blurted out. "My brother's a poet?"

Pierce nodded as he got a glass down from a cabinet.

Charlotte came up behind him and hugged him. "Where were you two? I missed you."

He turned in her embrace and kissed her cheek. "We got something to eat."

His wife looked up at him, faintly smiling, surprised. "Just the two of you?"

"We had a talk."

She began to say something, then stopped herself. Looking over her shoulder, she saw Caitlin was paging through a catalogue that had arrived in the mail. Charlotte lifted herself on her toes and whispered in her husband's ear, "That was wonderful last night. Unbelievable."

He smiled and gave her another kiss.

Pierce was shocked at how easy it all was. Really, he thought, it couldn't be any easier.

ON MONDAY MORNING, Pierce telephoned all the clients he had seen the week before. Though most tried to put him off, by noon he had scheduled follow-up visits with all but two. Lou was surprised when told about the trip. "You just got back Friday. Why don't you work the phone instead?" But Pierce sensed his manager's relief that he was going on the road again.

Charlotte was disappointed when she learned he was leaving in the morning. "It's just that the weekend was so different. You and Tack, I mean, spending time together." He caught the blush that darkened her cheeks. "And you and me."

"It's only three days. I'll be back Thursday." She wanted to be touched, he knew, so he took her face in his hands. "Anyway, I'm not leaving yet," he said softly and let her kiss him.

Pierce had no doubts the trip would be a success. One had only to pay attention to the customer on the other side of the desk—the way he shifted his weight to relieve the constant pressure in his chest, his habit of fingering the eraser on his pencil, the distraction that clouded his concentration when asked about his family, the vanity of cuff links rather than buttons, the whining pitch of the factory behind him. And like Charlotte, like Tack, he would be grateful for the attention, grateful to the point of generosity.

In fact, by the time the salesman pulled into the motel parking lot Tuesday evening, two hundred miles from home, he already had three major orders in hand. The last plant manager he had met that afternoon, a woman, had even asked him to stay for dinner. Next time, he promised.

It had been a long day. Alone in the anonymous motel room, still in his gray suit, he lay on the bed and let his gaze fall upon the bureau, the television set, the bedspread, the framed prints screwed to the wall. But everywhere he turned, his intense stare blurred and slid along the surfaces of things, unable to find purchase, unable to penetrate the familiarity of a room he had known in its thousand different versions all his working life. A weariness he had not noticed breeding over the last few days settled upon him until, suddenly unable even to lift his head under its weight, he fell into dreamless sleep.

A horn in the parking lot woke him about ten. He was startled, unsure where he was. Patting dry the water he had splashed on his face to help him wake, he inhaled the caustic smell of the towel's bleached cotton. The familiar odor calmed him. He was hungry, he realized.

As he had often done in his years on the road, Pierce followed a winding path past a deserted swimming pool, glowering in the cold moonlight, to the motel's lounge. Without thinking, he ordered a Manhattan, his regular drink. When the bartender told him the kitchen was still open, he declined a menu and simply asked for the only thing he ever ordered in a bar, steak and fries.

Well after midnight, he stood in front of his door, holding up his key to check it against the room number and then painstakingly fitting it into the lock. He barely got his clothes off before he collapsed into a deep, drunken sleep.

Though he succeeded in persuading one firm to upgrade, grudgingly, to a more advanced system, three other visits the next day yielded nothing. And Thursday, he had no luck at all.

When he pulled up to his house that evening, the curtains were already drawn. He turned off the ignition and leaned back against the headrest. Pierce was exhausted, the elation of his first day's successes having soured into a morose hopelessness as the failures had mounted over the following two days. Not even bothering to take his things out of the trunk, he unlocked the front door and sat down on the sofa.

The television was on, but the room was empty. The family was probably in the kitchen, or upstairs.

By the time Caitlin bounced down the stairs a few minutes later, Pierce was already stretched out on the sofa, sound asleep. Charlotte, kissing him on the forehead, kept the children out of the living room and let him sleep where he was.

Pierce woke in the middle of the night, confused and agitated, unsure how he had gotten there, where the blanket that covered him had come from. As he sat upright on the comfortable old sofa, holding his head in his hands, he remembered, with embarrassment, the listless presentations he had made to impatient executives earlier that day, the fumbled answers to their questions, the distracted explanations of why he had returned only a week after his first visit. He thought of the long, numb drive home just hours ago and of his clothes and samples still in the trunk.

Pierce climbed the stairs, holding his shoes. He felt each step sag, barely, under his weight. He heard the whispered breaths of the three sleepers. He saw, above a dim night lamp, the imperfections of a wall. But each quaver of light, each flutter of sound, each warble of wood beneath his body were syllables of a language he seemed almost to recognize but could no longer quite remember how to speak.

WHEN HE AWOKE the next morning to the clanging alarm, Pierce silenced the clock without opening his eyes. Charlotte, snuggling against him for his warmth, nestled her bare thigh between his legs. His hand curved, by habit, along the slope of her hip.

"The kids won't be up for another half hour," Charlotte whispered shyly, expectantly.

Afterward, the familiar scent of her hair nearly lulled him back to sleep as they curled in their sticky cocoon. Yet when she finally disentangled her body from his to wake Caitlin and Tack, he caught the impatience in her voice.

"I'm sorry," he mumbled, not sure what he had done wrong.

"It's my fault," she insisted crossly. "I should have let you sleep. You're still tired."

His children, too, seemed disappointed as they watched him across the breakfast table, but what they expected of him he could not imagine.

At work, though, Lou was beaming when Pierce stepped out of the elevator. "We got those orders you faxed Tuesday. How did you do it? Severn Brothers hasn't given us a nickel's worth of business in three years. And TrimCo—they didn't even want a catalogue the last time I talked to them."

"I had a good day."

"A good day?" Lou laughed, following Pierce to his desk. "You even sold a shipment to that son of a bitch at Southern Equipment."

"It's a woman there now," he explained, trying to remember her name.

Lou settled into a chair beside Pierce's desk. "So how'd you do at W&I yesterday? You must've cleaned up with that guy they've got running the place."

"No, nothing doing there. It's between seasons for them."

His boss's smile faded. "You're kidding? You sell TrimCo, but Huey Jenkins turns you down?"

Pierce shrugged.

"And the others?"

"Tennecon's upgrading to PV-7."

"But what about StanBob, DJ Fabrication, old man Higgins at Moreland-Wilkes?"

Pierce shrugged again.

"Well," Lou sighed, "an order's an order, even from a little guy like Tennecon." He had trouble getting out of his chair and leaned heavily on the edge of the desk, grimacing. "Anyway, that was good work on Tuesday. It really helped."

Pierce watched the old man take a few steps and then stop, catching his breath. "You OK, Lou?"

Without turning around, the sales manager held up his hand and nodded. "No problem," he puffed.

Pierce leaned back in the wooden swivel chair. He felt mired in something that was hardening, and he could not escape the sense it was his own life that was closing around him.

He imagined himself a fish that had leapt into the bright clarity of thin air and then flopped back into the sea, sinking into his own murky world as the water closed around the wound he had ripped in its surface—the water first perturbed, then pulsing, then still and seamless all the way to the horizon, where, he had learned, the blue ocean curled back on itself as a blue sky.

And as the light around him continued to cloud, like air thickening into water, Pierce decided he would leave work early that evening as the exhausted autumn sun descended among the rusting warehouses and deserted junkyards that lined the western approaches to the city. He would circle his neighborhood until the daylight dwindled, pulling up in front of his house as darkness fell. And he would turn his face to the great window in the desolate hope that his wife, bent over knife and fork and spoon beneath a chandelier of crystal shards, had not yet drawn the curtain.

A Battlefield in Moonlight

A HAND CAKED with mud dragged a body behind it out from under a heap of corpses. The little man, whose hand was pulling his whole body free of the grisly tangle of arms and legs and torsos like a spider pulling a paralyzed beetle from its lair, had lain unconscious for hours and hours. Now, nearly midnight, he had awakened. Grasping what he took to be a branch but was, in fact, the rigid foreleg of a horse half buried in the thick mud, he tugged his ankles from the indifferent grip of the dead.

Sitting up, still dazed, he looked around him. Banners of pale clouds shredded the moonlight, which fell in yellow strips on bodies and broken wheels and row after row of heads on sticks. He rubbed his face, wincing when his fingers brushed a long gash across his forehead. The moonlight crawled across the field as the clouds raced across the dark sky.

Suddenly, he saw a stand of pikes topped with heads just a few yards to his left. He sat in the mud, staring at them. One of the heads, toward the back of the little group, was still wearing its hat. The man recognized none of them.

Tilting his ears a bit, he thought he heard a murmuring. He turned around and for the first time saw the imperial camp massed on the hill, its fires blazing, the air laden with the musk of its distant songs. He stiffened, like a rabbit catching the vague rumor of unsheathed claws rasping on dry grass. Alert, the man swelled with such pain that he could not tell where he had been wounded.

He knew he had no time for pain or thirst or even fear. Pitching onto his knees, he began to crawl toward the forest that skirted the field. He could see it, beckoning him, two hundred yards beyond the heads he didn't recognize. He had gone only a few feet when the murmuring seemed to him to have grown louder. He looked behind him, like a dog checking its tail, but he saw no one. He crawled farther, weaving his way through the upright pikes and spears. Now the murmuring seemed to surround him. He stopped.

He knew where the sound was coming from before he even looked up. The moonlight still shone upon the heads. He turned and felt as if he were falling as he watched the trembling lips of one of the beheaded.

He should keep going, he knew. But the murmuring of the heads was so plaintive, so desolate, he could not abandon them. Kneeling before the one with the hat, he tried to make out what it was saying. He thought he heard "what" or "why"; it was some kind of question, he was almost sure. And the others, when he listened, were saying the same thing. He imagined that across the moonlit battlefield, all the heads were softly moaning the same word. But what was it? he wondered.

Looking over his shoulder, he saw no imperial troopers, no patrols on the perimeter of the field. The sentries were far up the hill. The rebellion must be over, he thought. He crawled to another head and, crouching, put his ear to the cracked and mumbling lips. His eyes widened as the word drifted down the canals of his understanding.

Water. He listened again. Yes, now he was sure. The heads were crying out for water.

He crawled back to the heap of bodies from which he had emerged. Furiously pulling corpse from corpse, he found a canteen still slung around the neck of one of the dead.

Crouching, half running, he returned to the heads, whose moan was rising like wind in an olive tree. The little man uncorked the canteen and was about to raise it to the lips of the head with the hat when he stopped and first took a long draught himself. Then, lifting the water to the head, he sprinkled a few drops on its lips. A black tongue slid out of the mouth like an eel from a crevice. The head rolled its eyes as if blind. Taking a deep breath, the man poured the water over its lips. It drank greedily as the water gushed out from its severed neck down into a muddy puddle around the base of the spear upon which it had been set.

The man pulled the canteen away. More clearly, though no more loudly, the head began again to beg for water. The little man, looking all around him at the hundreds of murmuring heads, saw the futility of his pity.

Perhaps it will rain for them, he thought, as he corked the canteen and crawled toward the dense forest. But the clouds were scattered later that night by a strong southeastern wind, and the sun rose some hours later over a silent battlefield.

Do Me

"DO ME," SHE whispered into his ear, urgent and certain. She had slipped her hands into the velvet loops tied to the bars of her headboard, and he could feel her feet searching, straining for the two loops at the foot of the bed.

The lids closed slowly over her green eyes. Her face tensed, expectant.

David lifted himself up and kissed Claire's neck. He felt her flinch.

"What are you doing?" she objected, struggling to pull away.

David, thinking she was playing, smiled. "I'm making love to you."

"That's not what I want," she whispered gravely. "Not that."

Claire was trying to work a hand free of the soft cord twisted about her wrist. David reached up and slipped it loose. She took his hand in hers. He smiled again, happy that she would tutor him in how to please her. Since he had met her three weeks ago in the coffee shop near his house, all he thought about was how to please her. *This is good,* he told himself, *she trusts me.* "Show me what you want," he nodded, relaxing.

Claire tightened her grip on his wrist and smashed his open palm against her cheek.

She let go his hand; it floated away like the head of a snake that had struck without warning, the fingers curling back like fangs. Even in the dim light from the hallway that fell in a slash across her pillow, David could see the cheek darken as it flushed with blood.

"Are you crazy?" A startled anger serrated his words.

Claire's eyes were closing. She slipped her hand back into the velvet loop. "Do it again," she insisted, a smile dying on her lips.

"No." He edged back from her. "I don't want to hurt you. I want to make you happy."

Her voice was more breath than words. "Then do it again."

"I won't."

"Please," she entreated, her eyes still closed.

The blotched face inclined toward him, blind and straining for his answer.

"Don't you love me?" she pouted, opening her eyes.

IT HAD NOT been like this the first time, a few nights earlier. They were at his place, watching a movie on TV. She had dropped by after her exercise class at the university, where she was finishing a master's in English. Lying on the sofa, half asleep, they had loosened each other's clothes little by little, lazily, almost indifferently, not really expecting anything to happen. Claire snuggled against David, her head on his arm, her back to him. With his free hand, he flicked open the buttons of the purple flannel shirt she wore over her tank top. "You must be hot," he had said. He let his hand loll beside her breast for a few moments before he touched her. She reached behind her back and unbuckled his belt.

Afterward, still mostly dressed, as each fell away from the other, dazed, neither seemed sure what had even happened, so quickly had sleep thickened into desire and desire melted back into sleep.

But when they awoke an hour later, Claire resisted David's kisses. "This weekend," she promised as she took the keys from her purse.

⚘

CLAIRE HAD LEFT a message on David's answering machine. She was sorry about the way the weekend had gone. She wanted to talk about it.

David hesitated to return her call. She was crazy. How else could you explain it, wanting a man to beat her? He hit the erase button.

There was nothing in the refrigerator when he was ready for dinner; he had forgotten to stop at the grocery on his way home. Now, though, he was too hungry to shop, so he went out for pizza. But when he returned after eating, the red light on his answering machine was blinking again.

It was Claire. She was going to stop by when she got out of her Early Moderns seminar around nine. He should have been annoyed, he knew, her dropping over without giving him a choice about it, but—he guiltily admitted to himself—he was glad she was coming. He missed her. Maybe he would turn out to be an idiot for letting her in, but he couldn't wait to see her.

Watching the clock, David tried to correct work sheets his students had filled out for homework, inserting missing semicolons between independent clauses. He reread the first of the twenty items he had written for the exercise: "The club is missing four thousand dollars, the club's treasurer is also missing."

It was difficult to concentrate; he kept thinking about Claire. He had seen her three or four times at Café Caffeine before he worked up the nerve to speak to her. He liked how still she was, reading a book or just sipping her coffee in the corner of the courtyard, ruffled palm fronds bowing behind her, sparrows pecking pastry crumbs at her feet.

The girls that he taught—fourteen years old, fifteen, sixteen—
would come tumbling into the coffee shop after school, always a knot
of them hanging on one another, arms entwined, shoving shoulder to
shoulder, scuffing their shoes, shrieking with laughter or hoots of
derision. And when they spied him against the wall, immersed in his
newspaper with a child's cup of espresso in front of him, a tiny chaff
of lemon rind poised on the lip of his saucer, they would stand smiling
at him, shushing one another's nervous laughter, until he looked up
over the top of the paper and nodded to them, "Girls." Then, giggling
foolishly, they would scatter to the courtyard with their tan glasses of
iced coffee and caffe latte.

In fact, it was as he had watched the girls gather chairs around an
outside table a month or two ago, still teasing one another and sneak-
ing sly glances at their teacher, that he had first noticed Claire.
Engrossed in a book, she seemed unaware of the flock of teenagers
that had descended on the table beside hers. He was moved by her
solitude, upon which even his raucous students were unable to in-
trude. Faced with such grace, as he described it to himself, he was not
surprised to feel a twinge of shame at his ridiculous vanity in having
savored the flirtations of the awkward girls, who continued to flash
shy smiles at their young teacher.

He reread another sentence on the work sheet: "When the captain
returned to the bridge of the ship, the battle already had been lost."
They would have trouble with that one, the weaker students. The correct items were always the most difficult for them. He tried to guess
who would get it wrong, who would introduce an error into the complex sentence. Dempsey, certainly, and Garifalo. He closed his eyes,
imagining the blue grid of little boxes in his grade book and, neatly
inked along the left margin, the names that descended in alphabetical
order. Morrison, he remembered, Morrison wouldn't stand a chance.
And Reichert, of course, that poor little thing.

He had caught her in first period that morning, the silly girl, filling
loose-leaf pages with the name of her beloved. But when he saw

whose name she had copied over and over again in her extravagant scrawl, the teacher had returned the green binder to the mortified student with a sigh of exasperation as her only reprimand.

WHEN CLAIRE GOT into her car in the gravel parking lot behind Averill Hall, she turned on the heater in the rusty Datsun. The rattle of its thin, sour breath, wheezing through the vents, promised little comfort. But then, sitting with her tight skirt hiked over her knees to drive, the woman felt the damp warmth beneath the dashboard, like a dog's panting, all along the inside of her clammy thighs. She opened her legs.

The hum of the engine soothed her as the car followed the empty streets to David's house. She wanted it to work between them. She wouldn't lie to herself about that—not this time. And if that meant changes, then things would simply have to change.

When she turned onto his block, though, she did not stop in front of his house. She kept driving. Only after a long loop around the neighborhood did she finally park before the well-tended lawn, follow the stepping-stones through the chilled garden of pink and purple salvia, and knock lightly on David's front door.

"WOULD YOU LIKE some hot chocolate? It's getting cold out there."

Claire smiled. "With marshmallows?"

"Marshmallows?" David repeated hopelessly. "Let me go look."

She could tell he did not want to disappoint her. "You know," she called after him, "let's not have marshmallows. Too much sugar this late."

"Are you sure?"

Even though he was in the next room, she could hear his relief. He was a sweet boy. "No marshmallows," she said firmly as she swung open the kitchen door.

He was still searching through cabinets, pushing aside canisters and boxes of food.

"Let me help," she offered. "Where's a pot?"

David stooped and withdrew a saucepan from the oven. As he handed it to her, he apologized, "There's not enough storage space. That's the one thing wrong with this kitchen."

She poured milk into the pot and measured out the chocolate with a wooden spoon.

"You do it the old-fashioned way," David observed. "I always use the microwave."

The woman turned on the burner. "It tastes different like that."

As she stood beside the stove, stirring the darkening milk, David leaned against the sink. He didn't want to talk about it yet. "So how was your class?"

"Interesting," she nodded, not looking up from the pot. "We've been studying the Symbolists."

David vaguely remembered the movement. "Everything standing for something else, huh?"

She kept swirling the chocolate into the milk. "More like everything hinting there is something else."

The steam was rising now. David moved next to Claire. The simmering milk frothed against the hot metal of the pot. "Looks like it's ready."

"Maybe," she said softly. Suddenly, her finger darted into the scalding liquid. Before he could say anything, she held it up to his lips. "Taste," she whispered, her face pale.

He grasped her hand and shook his head, sighing. But then he took the finger in his mouth.

DAVID DIDN'T EXPECT to see Claire the next evening; she had a paper due in Eighteenth-Century Prose and Poetry. A message from her earlier in the day had explained that she was half finished with *Pamela* and couldn't put it down. "Just like Pope," she boasted on the answering machine. "You know he read the whole thing in one night? By candle."

David couldn't understand her enthusiasm for the novel, or Pope's, for that matter—he had read an excerpt of the beleaguered Pamela's letters in a survey course—but he was glad Claire was occupied. He needed time to think.

In her visit Monday, she had evaded his questions, playfully at first, then sulkily as he persisted. When he had pressed her, she closed herself to him, hunching her shoulders and averting her face from his gaze. He was hurting her, he realized all at once, and so he had relented.

Now, though, David determined to get to the bottom of the thing—even if it did hurt. For her sake, he insisted. Surely she was searching for a way out. He would help her find a way. His confidence swelling into elation, he poured himself a third glass of wine.

When he recognized her scratchy knock at his door, a few minutes later, he was pleased. Now that he knew what he had to do, he was glad that she had decided to drop by.

Claire couldn't stop talking about *Pamela*. "I just can't believe how good it is," she bubbled.

David tried to shift the conversation, shrugging off the novel as "interesting." But Claire continued to come back to the story. Only when the man began to kiss her did she smile and stop.

"Let's go in the bedroom," she said, already unbuttoning her blouse.

She was naked and kneeling on the bed before he had even taken off his shirt. "I can't hurt you, you know," David sighed, still standing.

"I don't want to talk about it." There was something dry, almost raspy in her voice. "Just come to bed."

"No." David was surprised by how forcefully it came out, so he repeated it more gently. "No, we have to talk." He lowered himself into the armchair beside the window and flicked on the reading lamp next to it.

The woman recoiled from the light, wrapping herself in the bed-spread. "About what?"

David was already exasperated. "You don't know what I want to talk about?"

"What's your problem?" she sighed wearily. "I can't make you do what you don't want to do."

"But it's coming between us. You're asking for something I can't give you."

"Won't give me," she corrected him.

"No, that's not true." He took another sip of the wine he had carried into the bedroom, and his face flushed with its heat. "I can't hit you."

Claire sensed she had hold of something inside that made him twitch. She squeezed it. "It's nothing to be ashamed of. You're afraid, that's all."

"I'm not afraid. It's just wrong."

Her laughter jostled the bedspread that covered her. A fold fell free, exposing a breast. "Wrong?" she mocked. "What's wrong with pleasing a woman?"

David had never before been laughed at by a woman in his bed. He looked down, throbbing with indignation, and saw what small hands he had. Claire was still laughing to herself, and when he glanced at her, he thought he detected a sneer deforming her smile.

Who the fuck does she think she is? he thought as he finished off the wine in his glass.

"Yeah, have another drink," she scoffed, "maybe then you'll grow some balls."

He stood up and drew his belt free of his pants.

"Oh, what are you going to do? Beat me?" She laughed again, more cruelly, and let the bedspread drop to the mattress. "Go ahead, do it," the naked woman taunted. She pitched forward, flat across the bed, and closed her eyes in contempt. "Do me," she dared him.

Claire was still laughing when the first blow fell across her back. She turned her face to the man and saw the belt whipping toward her again, like a serpent striking from a tree. And she felt it lash her a third time before she could even raise her hands in defense.

Standing over her huddled, naked body, David saw the three stripes rising as long, raw welts across her back. The belt dropped from his numb hand. He fell to his knees and embraced her, kissing a face already salty with tears. "I'm sorry, sorry," he repeated, trembling with what he hoped was shame.

"Again," she whispered in his ear, her breath hot from crying. "Again."

IF IT HADN'T BEEN for the likelihood of bumping into some of his students there, David would have met Claire at Café Caffeine. He hadn't seen her in almost a week, since that last night at his place, but even as he had put off calling her, he was learning how deep within him his desire for the woman had rooted. Her relief that it was him on the phone pleased the young man enormously when he finally called to invite her to dinner at a restaurant across town. They would be able to talk there, he felt sure. They would be able to work it out.

The dinner was better than they were used to at the student diners near the university. Claire was in a playful mood. Maybe it was the wine, David thought. When the waiter had taken their order for dessert and coffee, he slid his chair a little closer to Claire's and asked her to explain it all to him. "How did it get started, the stuff in bed?"

She sobered quickly. "I don't want to talk about it."

"Is it something from when you were little? Did something happen to you?"

"What difference does it make where it comes from? It's just the way I am."

"But that's the point. You don't have to live with it."

Claire was getting angry. "I like it." David started to object, but she cut him off. "I like it very much."

He tried to be calm. "We've got to work this out. It's going to wreck us."

"Well, if it wrecks us . . . ," Claire began harshly, as if she had been through this before, but then she softened. "I don't want it to do that. I want to be with you."

David had not realized he had been waiting for her to say that. "I want to be with you, too. But I can't go on hurting you every time we make love. I just can't do it."

"Why not?" Now Claire was intense. "It worked last week, with the belt. That was all right, wasn't it? I mean afterward, for you."

"No, it wasn't all right. I was drunk that night."

There was an edge to her voice. "You weren't that drunk."

He knew she was right. "I couldn't even look at you when we woke up." He took a breath. "I was ashamed of myself."

"Why should it bother you so much if I'm the one asking for it?"

David shook his head. "We have to find another way."

Claire stared at the table. In a circle around her water glass, a stain was darkening the pink linen cloth. "There is no other way," she said quietly.

❦

IN CLAIRE'S ARMS, David had yielded, little by little, to accommodations of her desires. It could not go on like this, he insisted to himself. Yet it did.

It was all an act, the man protested whenever he confronted his growing guilt. He pretended to hurt the woman, and she pretended to be hurt. None of it was real. He had guarded his emotions ever since the night he had struck her with his belt; he was always in control.

But he could not control his feelings for her, which deepened day by day. They had been seeing each other for nearly two months. They had begun to talk about the future, what would happen when Claire finished her degree. She wanted him to meet her mother at Christmas.

He knew bringing it up again was pointless. Claire seemed to assume that he had resigned himself to the arrangement.

"You know, I read something in a poem the other day that made me think of us," she said tenderly one night, brushing the hair from his eyes. "An instrument grows into its music."

David couldn't tell if she was talking about herself, or about him.

❦

THOUGH IT WAS well after midnight, David couldn't sleep. "We can't go on like this."

Claire had stopped taking his occasional objections seriously. "We're doing fine," she sleepily assured him. "I've never been so happy."

"I want you to be happy. But I can't keep doing it."

The woman put her head on his shoulder and stroked his chest, following the grain of his flesh. "Tomorrow we'll talk about it," she hushed him. "But go to sleep now. It's late."

David was too restless to sleep. "The thing is, I really wish I could do what you want."

"I know, sweetheart. Now go to sleep." Claire snuggled against his chest.

"But how can I go on hurting you every night? That's not love."

His last word woke her. "Love?" In the distance, she could hear his heart beating. "Why can't it be love?"

Claire listened for an answer in the dark. After a few moments, she touched the man's face, but whichever way her hand moved, the stubble of his beard opposed her fingers.

The next morning, when she made the bed, Claire tucked the velvet loops under her mattress.

❦

CLAIRE LET HERSELF be loved as David preferred. But the man soon discovered, to his gnawing shame, that he had bound the woman more tightly than she had ever bound herself. Pinioned by the cords of his insistence, her scored flesh was slack to his fingers, numb to his lips. When she writhed beneath him, it was false, all of it.

After a few nights, disgusted with himself, he admitted his way would not work. "No more acting," he told her.

The gravity of what he said made her shiver. "I love you," she mouthed as David kneeled over her, his knees sinking into the spongy mattress.

"Do me," she whispered deep in her throat, raising her head up toward him even as the velvet bindings tautened around her wrists and ankles.

He couldn't help himself. He loved her.

She closed her eyes. She was waiting for him.

He was about to bring it down, his open hand, hard across her face. But then, as if his arm had been stayed at the last moment by a sudden realization, the hand began to tremble and fell, limp, against his naked thigh.

The man slipped the loops off the woman's ankles, then loosened her wrists from the bindings.

"It's OK," Claire sighed as she turned to the wall. "It's OK."

She felt him behind her, straining for something.

When she turned back to him, he had slipped his own hands and feet into the velvet loops. He lay exposed on the bed, bound to its four corners.

"Do me," David ordered her in a small and frightening voice.

"What?" Claire refused to understand.

"You do me," he repeated in a low, thick whisper.

She straddled him, furious, as if he were mocking her and felt her arm swell as it rose up over her head to strike him. "You son of a bitch," she hissed.

But then he closed his eyes, and the anger went out of her, even as her hand came down on his face.

Though David winced, he did not open his eyes. He could hear the woman, who swayed above him, weeping, and he felt a hot tear scald his chest.

"Again," the man insisted gently, desolately, "again."

The Torturer's Apprentice

THERE ONCE WAS a boy of good heart but meager prospects whose father apprenticed him to a torturer.

It was, unfortunately, a period of decline for the guild. The Inquisition was winding down, and the great witch trials were still a century away. It is true that, here and there, in Toledo, Cologne, Toulouse, Genoa, elderly masters of the trade still practiced their skills on those unlucky enough to run afoul of the authorities. But upon their deaths, the duchies and baronies and city-states and kingdoms declined, one after another, to fill their vacant posts. So, traveling on business or pilgrimage through the countryside, one more and more frequently encountered itinerant torturers bringing their expertise to the smaller jurisdictions of mountain villages and rural parishes. It was to such a journeyman that young Alain Macheret was apprenticed.

With twenty years of experience behind him in southern France and northern Spain, Guillem Vouze was well schooled in the art of persuasion. (He remembered with pride a Dominican in Barcelona who had once complimented him on his "eloquence in the rhetoric of the body.") His only weakness was his devotion to his craft. Unslakable in his thirst for knowledge of human physiology and tireless in his enthusiasm for the latest inventions of discomfort, he had indebted himself as his collection of tools grew. His expertise, in fact, was explained in whispers by the malicious and vengeful relatives of his confessed criminals and heretics as the fruit of secret experiments performed upon corpses by the torturer. He worried less, though, about such serious allegations and about the cost of his investments in more and more sophisticated machines than he did about the simple problem of hauling all his equipment over the rutted springtime roads and the frozen mountain passes of winter.

So when, on his regular circuit through the farming hamlets of Provence, he was approached by Alain's father seeking a craft for the boy, he quickly came to terms with the old man. Such a muscular youth could shoulder a great burden. Perhaps, it also occurred to the torturer, the boy might be trained to operate the basic functions of the machinery, freeing the master to concentrate on more intricate applications of pain.

But though Guillem would not admit it to himself, the idea of a traveling companion to share the rainy distances between villages and to commiserate on the paltry accommodations of the parish houses may have influenced his decision to accept the apprentice. The demands of the road and the fearsome reputation of torturers had intervened on the few occasions when romance might have bloomed in Guillem's life; distracted by his career, he had not recognized the dull ache of loneliness that throbbed in his heart. But offered a kind of son in young Alain, he did not hesitate to embrace the opportunity to escape his solitude.

The apprentice's education was thorough. Many of the techniques Guillem patiently explained on their long journeys have been lost to us; the secrets of the guild were inviolate, and manuals would have been of little use to the illiterate practitioners of the craft. So one can only guess at the body of knowledge bestowed upon the young man by the torturer. Surely there were stories of the fabled masters, anecdotes of odd experiences, tales of inadvertent discoveries of techniques. But the bedrock of his education must have been a comprehensive study of anatomy, a thorough training in the mechanics of a torturer's tools, and a demanding drill of procedures and applicable laws of church and state. Considering the debt under which his master labored, Alain must have had at his disposal a full panoply of contemporary instruments of torture. He certainly would have had the opportunity to tighten with his own hands the screw of a garrote, to test the pulleys of a strappado, to unbuckle the iron girdle of a twisting stork, to set a tongue lock between jaw and collarbone, perhaps even to clean the bloody spikes of an Inquisitor's chair.

Alain's education continued for some years under the increasingly fond supervision of his master. Though each spring their circuit would return the two torturers to Alain's remote village and the joyful embrace of his large family, the boy came more and more to think of Guillem with the respect he had once accorded his father.

Certainly a bond had been forged between apprentice and teacher in the smoky dungeons that served as the boy's classrooms. Alain had grown up to the pitiful squeals of slaughtered sheep and the rough butchery of hogs in the yard; he had watched the women render goats' heads and pigs' feet to jelly in the village's great pot and had licked from his mother's fingers the thick blood she had boiled for sausage. But the cry he elicited from the first heretic on whom he was allowed to tighten a leg brace echoed in him for days afterward. Annoyed at first by the boy's squeamishness, Guillem came to appreciate his apprentice's gentleness. He had often sensed that cruelty was the enemy of the torturer. In fact, cruelty seemed to him a kind of arrogance that a professional would disdain; it was an intoxicant of amateurs. Though he knew the boy would harden soon enough to the pathetic entreaties of the accused, he hoped the young man would never entirely cease to wince at the screams produced through his handiwork.

Guillem also admired the quiet religious faith that sustained his apprentice. Tested again and again through the cynical application of torture by avaricious clerics greedy for the land of the condemned, Guillem's own faith had shriveled. He, of course, still observed the Sabbath and the holy days, tithed what the clergy demanded, and honored the Virgin. But these were the empty practices of a faithless man. Though belief eluded him, Guillem was nonetheless moved by Alain's gentle charity. Who knows? Perhaps he secretly hoped that he might follow the boy back to God. None knew better than a torturer that without the comfort of religion, life is a vale of tears.

In their years together, Alain had grown to early manhood under the harsh rigors of the road, and the simple girls of the countryside mooned over his dark eyes and shy smile. Confined for life to their muddy fields and thatched huts, the girls bribed Alain with sweet milk and bread for stories of the great towns and markets through which he had passed.

But Alain, himself a simple and innocent farm boy, was unprepared when a young woman of Axat, a small town in the Pyrenees where the torturers had been marooned for a week by late snowfalls, offered the apprentice a sweeter temptation than a ladle of milk. Shocked by her whispered invitation, Alain preserved his innocence through prayer and through his infatuated devotion to another girl of the town whom he had glimpsed at Mass. Martine, the young woman who had failed once to seduce him, tried again the next day, this time threatening to make trouble for him if he refused. Foolishly, he told her that he loved another. The jealous young woman cursed him furiously. Alain, frightened, ran back to his master, whose questions he moodily ignored.

Martine, already experienced in the consequences of love, snared a little mouse whose burrow she knew. Crushing it against a stone, she smeared her thighs and stained her smock with its blood. Then, having rolled in the snow, she stumbled back to her home, dazed and weeping. Her sly refusal, at first, to allow her mother to examine her brought all the neighbors to her door before she at last relented and lifted her skirt for the old women. When her father pushed past the women back into the house, Martine again refused, at first, to divulge anything. But when the big man threatened to beat her, she quickly confessed that the torturer's apprentice had raped her.

Only the presence of the parish priest in the rectory where the two visitors were staying saved Alain from the violence of the townsfolk. But within days, the young man had been delivered to the authorities at Quillan for trial.

Guillem had served the bustling town of Quillan for years. In fact, he had developed a polite acquaintance with the jurisdiction's magistrate, Bertran d'Uzes. Though he knew he could expect no considerations from the judge, the torturer comforted his apprentice with his confidence that the learned jurist would uncover the truth. Alain insisted that he was an innocent in God's hands and so feared nothing.

Guillem, troubled by the boy's behavior the afternoon the townsmen had stormed the rectory, was not certain of his innocence. Returning from a walk in the snowy fields where Martine was to testify that he had forced himself upon her, the usually happy and open young man refused to talk, acting as if he were ashamed of something. But Guillem's affection for the boy and his distrust of the strange girl weighed more heavily than his doubts.

Presented with Martine's accusation, Bertran d'Uzes accepted the witnesses' corroboration of her story as a legitimate half-proof, but in the absence of an eyewitness, he insisted upon the Queen of Proofs, a confession. The judge solemnly ordered Alain Macheret to be put to the question. Bertran directed the court's torturer, Guillem, to apply the strappado to his apprentice for the length of a recitation of the creed. Alain would be put to the question three times.

Guillem, profoundly distressed by the judge's decision to employ the strappado, had hoped for the rope tortures reserved for women and children. (He still saw Alain as the young boy waving farewell for the first time to his tearful mother.) But the seriousness of the charge and the muscular frame of the young man condemned him to the Queen of Torments.

A priest and a guard led Alain to the room where Guillem had hoisted the creaking pulleys of the strappado. The apprentice, so often having assisted in the deployment of the device, slipped his own hands into the noose held behind his back. Pulling the lines taut, Guillem watched the twisted arms lift above the boy's bent back. The moan that slipped from Alain's lips when his feet left the floor and the wretched sigh that escaped with each breath as he dangled above them tormented Guillem. The judge, reverently reciting his creed, would not be hurried. As soon as the priest responded to Bertran's final words with "Amen," the torturer lowered his flushed and agonized apprentice to the ground. Crumpled on the cold floor, Alain raised his head to whisper his innocence into the ear of the judge, who had begged him to confess.

Intoning for a second time the formula of the question, the magistrate nodded to his torturer to raise the accused. Again Bertran recited the creed. Over the judge's head, moans yielded to desperate screams as each shift of Alain's weight strained beyond endurance another strap of muscles. Guillem grew pale.

Bringing the boy down too quickly at the priest's "Amen," Guillem heard the body smack against the stone floor like a sack of turnips dropped from a loft. The magistrate was dismayed but stooped to ask the accused again to declare his guilt and save himself from further torment.

Guillem almost hoped that Alain would confess, but the judge raised himself up and for the last time repeated the formula of the question.

The torturer had seen it before. A man would endure the agony of two flights in the strappado. He would tell himself that if he could simply keep silent for a few moments more the judge would declare him innocent. He could return to the arms of his wife. He could sleep in his own bed that very night. He could escape the dreadful executioner, who waited to exact punishment for the crime of which he had been accused. But swaying gently above his tormentors as muscle after muscle was exhausted into spasm, as cramps contorted his body into more and more painful postures at the end of the rope, he forgot his wife and his bed. He even forgot his fear of death. There was no future, no past—only the hideous present. The cry of confession that would interrupt the judge's prayer was very different from the screams that had preceded it: never once had the torturer heard a judge ask the accused to repeat the low moan of submission. Everyone in the room recognized its meaning immediately. The torturer would lower the whimpering body, the judge would already be entering the verdict in the court's log, and the priest would celebrate the divine intervention that had cast the light of truth upon the shadowy crime of this condemned sinner.

With each tug of the lines, Guillem's experienced hands could feel the effect of the first two flights on Alain's body. Where there had been taut resistance in the beginning, now at the other end of the pulleys and ropes hung deadweight. But not the most horrific apparition from the grave could have produced the chilling moans that issued from the body floating above their heads. Even the judge was unsettled, stumbling in his creed at the sudden bursts of screams that punctuated the agony of young Alain.

Guillem could not stand another moment of the suffering. He had secretly tutored his apprentice in how to hold the body to lessen the effects of the strappado, but now the boy was adrift in a sea of pain and could not remember how to swim. While the judge continued to enunciate with the most careful deliberation each syllable of the creed, Guillem surreptitiously let out one line and drew in another to ease the pressure on Alain's back. It was difficult to manipulate the device without attracting the attention of the others, but they were transfixed by the ecstasy of pain above them. All at once, the boy seemed to awaken as if from a dream. He suddenly shifted his weight just as Guillem was jerking a line taut. Beneath the piercing scream,

Guillem heard the tendons snap, the muscles rip away from the bone, the joints pop from their sockets. Then he heard the priest say, "Amen."

He lowered the boy as gently as they must have lowered the Savior from the cross. The judge bent to the broken body and asked whether Alain wished to confess. The young man with a single word refused.

In open court, the innocence of Alain Macheret was declared. Martine's father was ordered to pay the boy blood money for the false accusation of his daughter. Martine herself eventually was consigned by her family to the convent at Foix, where, after some brief notoriety as a visionary, she contracted a fever and died.

No one but Guillem was aware of his role in the crippling injury to his apprentice. The boy's left arm hung slack as he dragged his leg after him down the dusty summer roads, and his drooping shoulder gave him the appearance of a hunchback. Though he still had the face of an angel, girls turned away from him as he hobbled past their farms. Parents began to threaten unruly children with a midnight visit from the disfigured torturer. The mere sight of him at trials would sometimes persuade the guilty to confess without being put to the question. And everywhere he traveled, he edified the faithful with the tale of how he had been preserved from condemnation by a just and loving God.

Guillem was confounded by the faith of the young man, but to dispute that faith would have been to put himself in jeopardy with the Inquisitors and their agents. He felt guilty about the crippling of Alain, but having discovered in Quillan that pity was as dangerous a distraction to a torturer as cruelty, he learned to ignore the scrape of his apprentice's boot against the floor.

And Never Come Up

Was there a story?

There was always a story.

Did you write this one down?

I've written them all down.

Will you read it to me?

It wasn't really his story. I thought it was. I thought it had something to do with him—or one of his shipmates, at least. That it had happened on a boat he knew. But then I was reading to my son one night, and there it was in this book of sea stories.

Exactly the same?

No, just the idea. All the details were different.

Stories get passed on. Maybe your father heard it somewhere.

Maybe. But he made me believe it was no story. I thought it was true.

Why?

Because of what he said after he told it to me.

Read it to me. Please.

. If you like.

The freighter was three days out of New Orleans on its run to Panama when the wife and the daughter of the ship's captain both succumbed, in the space of a few hours, to a fever from which they had suffered since their first day at sea.

As the bodies of the handsome woman and the little girl were wound in canvas for burial, old salts, shaking their heads, repeated to the younger hands the ancient injunction against sailing with women. "It's a terrible shame, but we're lucky it weren't worse," the bo's'n confided to the third mate, who had brought the sorrowful news to the bridge.

The captain, with twenty years experience of the vagaries of the sea, was not so bold a man as to have been indifferent to the superstition. In fact, he had for a year denied the repeated entreaties of his daughter to take her with him on a voyage. Only as a special birthday present to this child whom he adored without measure had he relented. His wife, delighted that at least once in her life she would not have to bid farewell to her beloved husband from the edge of a dock, spurred him to live up to his promise.

And so, on the second of September, with the assurance of the harbormaster that the Gulf threatened no hurricane at the moment, the captain ushered aboard his ship the child and her mother. Having slipped its moorings, the freighter nosed down the Mississippi under the command of a river pilot. At the mouth of the river, the pilot disembarked, remarking to his fellows when he had returned to Pilottown on the captain who had taken the whole family to sea. "He some crazy, huh?" the pilot's father observed.

Already the woman and her child were faint with their illness. "It's to be expected," the captain told them, and he tried to comfort them with tales of his own seasickness on his first trip out. But the onset of fever late that afternoon alarmed him; they were not seasick.

The ship, of course, had no doctor, but the second mate did what he could to ease their discomfort. When they grew too weak to swallow the aspirins he had taken from the medicine locker, he crushed the pills beneath his thumb in the bowl of a spoon and added a few drops of water so they might drink the medicine. But their decline was so steady and seemed to him so certain that he had shaken his head over them a good day before they finally died.

The captain, having seen his share of death in the war, trembled but held his composure as his first officer read from his Kingspoint manual the liturgy for burial at sea. The crew, unpracticed in this drill, stumbled in sliding the bodies over the side. The ship's navigator, as required by maritime custom, shot the sun and fixed the location of the burial, noting it on the ship's chart and conveying it to the captain for entry in the log.

The remainder of the voyage was uneventful. One of the sailors got into a bit of trouble on shore leave, but the local authorities were glad to release him to the custody of an officer of the ship.

The freighter, now laden with coffee, retraced its route back to New Orleans. Two days out of Panama, in the middle of the third watch, an officer called the captain to the bridge.

Fifty yards off the starboard bow, the water rose up in the shape, vaguely, of two figures—one somewhat taller than the other. The captain dropped his binoculars. "Sir," the navigator nearly whispered, "we're very close to the spot, very close."

As the ship slid past, the watery figures trembled in the bright sunlight. Finally, the watch saw the two columns of water collapse after the stern had passed them.

By the time the ship docked in New Orleans, the captain had been locked in his cabin. Orderlies from St. Simon's Asylum led the man down the gangplank in restraints.

New Orleans is one of the great ports of the world. The story easily found its way to the pages of the local papers. Intrigued by the tale, the *Item* sent a photographer on the Panama run when the ship embarked a week later.

Again two watery figures rose up.

In a quiet dinner at Antoine's a few days after the photo's publication, in the face of a threatened strike by the seafarers' union, the owners of the four lines that traded with Panama agreed to reroute their ships to a more easterly course. The new route they plotted that night has been followed for the last half century.

In all that time, no ship has passed within ten miles of the location fixed by the navigator that melancholy afternoon. Whether the sea remains calm there or whether a mother and her daughter have risen up like pillars of water each day for the last fifty years, no man can say.

That's your version?

That's how I wrote it down.

But that's not how he told it.

It's overwritten, you think. I worried about that.

No, not at all. But from what you've said, I just can't imagine that's how he told it. When did you write it?

A year ago. Then a few days ago, again. But no, it's not the way he told it. To be the same, it would be whispered so close to your face you could smell the breath that carried it, but in darkness so black you couldn't even see the lips that were telling it.

You're resorting to poetry again.

No, no, I'm not. That's exactly how it was, the night I heard the story. It's the absolute truth.

How is that possible? Where were you?

We were deep in the marsh, back down one of those winding canals off the ship channel. We'd been hauling in speckled trout hand over foot for better than an hour when they stopped biting. It was already nearly three, so my father tried to start the engine. He pulled on the cord till I thought he would rip the top off the motor, but it didn't even cough.

You'd been fishing?

Yeah, we had a little fourteen-foot plywood runabout my father and grandfather had built, the kind with fiberglass tape at the seams. Everybody made their own in those days. My grandfather wasn't with us, though, out in the marsh. I think maybe he was already in the hospital by then.

How old were you?

I don't know. Nine. Maybe ten.

You were just a baby.

No, I wasn't a baby. I was ten years old.

Oh, you were a baby. Ten years old.

OK, I was a baby. We had this huge outboard on the back—my father won it somehow playing pinochle—and when you leaned on the throttle, the boat just about jumped out of the water. So we called it the *Mullet.*

Mullet?

It's this little fish that jumps out of the water when something big is chasing it. You can't catch them with a hook. Their mouths are too small.

So what did your father do?

Bobbing there in our little boat, Daddy changed the spark plugs, cleaned the lines, checked the pumps, went through the whole drill. But when he popped the cover back on and tugged the cord again—nothing. We were stuck. And hunkered back in the marsh the way we were, we hadn't seen another boat in a couple of hours. It was so hot by then, if your hand brushed a cleat you got burned. So there weren't many damn fools still out.

Then what did your father do?

What he always did. He pulled a bottle out of the ice chest.

But what about you? You must have been frightened, a little child like you.

There used to be a saying around here when I was a boy: "Nobody but God can whup my daddy, and God better watch his step." As long as Daddy was leaning back against the bow drinking Dixies, it was just another fishing trip as far as I was concerned. I knew Mama would be upset, our being late and all—and I was worried about that because I knew what would happen if she made too much of a fuss when we got home. But afraid of being stranded out in the marsh? I didn't have the slightest idea how much trouble we were in.

Your father knew what he was doing, didn't he?

Sure. In all the times we went out there, I never once saw him check a chart, and anybody'll tell you what a labyrinth those canals are. Nothing but saw grass and water as far as you can see.

And your father had been a sailor, hadn't he?

Yeah, that's right. He was in the merchant marine until I was born and my mother made him come home. He sailed damn near everywhere. I don't know how many winter runs he made in the North Atlantic. The water's so cold that time of year, if you fall overboard, you're dead in twenty seconds. At least, that's what he used to tell me. He dodged submarines in the Pacific during the war, took a ship through the Suez, rode out a typhoon in the South China Sea.

He must have seen some things.

He said you could walk to shore on the backs of the sharks they were so thick in Manila Bay. In fact, he lost one of his shipmates when they were unloading in the Philippines near the end of the war. The idiot got drunk and decided to go for a swim, right there where they were anchored.

Didn't anybody try to stop him?

I asked my father about that once, when I was still small. That's the thing about sailors, he explained. They'll warn you off of trouble, but not a one of them will ever stop you. You want to take your boat out in weather like this? One of them will tell you, "Might get a little wet today." By which he means, "If you're damn fool enough to go out on a day like this, the crabs'll be scraping the flesh from your bones at the bottom of the sea before you're done." But nobody's going to stop you. It's your boat.

You don't have to be so grisly.

That's the way Daddy put it. He said deep down they all expected to drown sooner or later themselves, so they didn't see any point in going to a lot of trouble to keep someone from drowning sooner.

This is the kind of story your father told a ten-year-old?

Ten? He was telling me his stories before I went to school. They weren't any worse than fairy tales.

Crabs scraping the flesh from your bones?

Wolves eating up grandmothers and inviting children into their bed?

So what about the man who went swimming?

My father said his buddy hadn't been in the water half a minute before a shark took his legs. But it was quiet, he said; they never even saw the shark. The man rolled like a ship broaching—that's the way he always put it, and running in those Pacific convoys for two years, he saw plenty of ships broach—and the guy just bobbed there upside down for a moment or two, bloody stumps in the air, then slid under, gone.

There's really no need to—

He hated the Indian Ocean—the storms lasted so long down there they'd eat cold mess three days running because it was too rough for the cooks to make hot food. But you know what was the most dangerous thing he ever did at sea? Haul molasses from the Caribbean to the East Coast.

Molasses? What's so dangerous about that?

I'll tell you how dangerous it is. Molasses carried the highest premium for hazardous cargo. That's why he did it, for the money, the bonus. And we needed the molasses for explosives, so there was a lot of demand during the war.

But what's so dangerous about it?

It's heavier than water. If a ship was hit and went down, the molasses took everything with it to the bottom of the sea. Down where the crabs were waiting.

No survivors.

None. My father was a real sailor, all right. So he knew what he was doing on the water. Of course, he told me one night when he was good and drunk that the best advice he'd gotten in a dozen years at sea was from an old sailor on the first ship he sailed, the *Howard Hand-strom* I think it was. You've probably heard this saying before. "Never learn to swim—it only prolongs the drowning." I remember when he told me he took another swig of bourbon and then, with one eye open, swore, "But goddamn it, I already knew how to swim."

So what happened to you out in the marsh?

My father and I sat there till dusk. I tried fishing some, but the water was too hot and the tide was out. Daddy kept drinking. We had some kind of cheese spread my mother had made and soda crackers, so that was our dinner. Every once in a while, Daddy would stand up on the bench and look for another boat, but nobody else was still out, and we were too far off the channel to catch a tow with the shrimp boats coming in from the Gulf. He was still in a pretty good mood, though. After he'd taken a look, he would say, "I'd better send up a flare." And he'd unzip his pants and take a piss, standing up on the seat. I guess it was all the beer he'd been drinking.

And what about you?

I'd kept my Dodgers baseball cap on the whole day, and of course, we both were wearing long-sleeved shirts. But by the time the sky in the east began to turn purple, I'd had too much sun. Hot as it was and even though I was still wearing one of those big, old-fashioned life jackets, I started getting chills. Fever, I guess.

Keep a child out there all day on the water till he gets sick?

I was sick all right, but we had a bigger problem to deal with. I could already hear them lifting out of the grass before I could see them. At first, I thought it was an engine. Dizzy as I was, I stood up on the bench. I was sure we were saved. I was really proud, too. Daddy had fallen asleep in the bow. I was going to be the lookout that spied a boat and saved the crew. But there weren't any boats when I looked, just small dark clouds hovering, twitching over the mudflats. I didn't know what they were—smoke, fog? But as the roaring got louder, I looked down at my hands. They were seething with mosquitoes. It was weird, I hadn't felt a thing. Maybe it was the fever, I don't know, but I watched these bugs crawling all over themselves like it was somebody else's hands they were biting. And then, very calmly, I plunged both arms into the water. With my face close to the canal, the racket from all those little wings overhead was unbelievable. I reached behind me to shake my father awake by the leg. He didn't stir. That was when I began to be afraid. So I crawled beside him, and when I got close enough to see him in the dark, his face and neck were so thick with mosquitoes he looked like he had a black beard. I tried to call out to wake him, but my mouth was full of them before I could even say his name. I choked on mosquitoes, spitting them out into the water. My coughing woke him up. By then, they were in our eyes. I think my eyelids were starting to swell shut from all the bites. The next thing I knew, Daddy had thrown me overboard and jumped in beside me.

My God.

He was spitting out the bugs even as he shouted at me. He got his shirt off and threw it over my head like a little tent. Then I felt him underwater, loosening my life jacket and working my own shirt off. I couldn't see him till he came right up in front of my face under the tent of his shirt. "Vicious little bastards, aren't they?" he shouted at me even though he was just inches away. And then he said, "Here, you put your own shirt over your head when I tell you to." His hand brought up the sopping shirt my mother had buttoned on me that morning when it was still dark outside. I remember it had cowboys with lariats all over it. I think they were on horseback. Daddy said the first thing we had to do was tie the sleeves in knots so the mosquitoes couldn't get in. And we had to make sure that the edges of our shirts stayed in the water.

You had your life vest on?

Yeah, of course. I wasn't allowed in the boat without a life jacket. Anyway, Daddy was working in the dark on all this. It had gotten pitch black under the shirt. The brim of my baseball cap kept the fabric off my face when Daddy submerged. He had helped me slip my shirt under his own. It was a much smaller little tent. I hadn't realized how big my father was. His shirt had been huge, but I could barely keep the edges of mine in the water. In fact, it was so dark it was hard to tell where the water began. My father said to keep dipping my head under so the shirt would stay wet. "They find you by your heat," he whispered, as if they might hear. "Stay wet and they won't know where you are." That worried me. I was afraid my fever would give us away. But the water was making me feel better.

That's horrifying.

It gets worse.

Worse?

Little by little, Daddy had felt his way along the edge of the boat until he found some footing on the bottom. He could stand with his head out of the water. He had tightened the straps on my life jacket and drawn his shirt over himself and me, so I was under two shirts. It was the strangest feeling, floating there in the darkness. I'd get panicked every now and then, when I couldn't hear him breathing—we were only a few inches apart. Then he'd talk to me, calm me down. I got used to it after a while, I guess, because I was slipping in and out of sleep, a few hours later, when something brushed my leg and made me jump. Like I said, Daddy was standing up, probably sunk to his ankles in the muck. That still left a good five feet of water. I asked him if he had felt anything. He hadn't. But just as he said no, something hit us both at the same time, coming between us, I think. Daddy staggered back a step or two, slipping on the bottom.

A shark?

Probably. You always saw them there, a fin slicing through the water out in the channel. You looked for a second fin following the first, that's how you could tell it was shark. Otherwise, it was just a dolphin with that horizontal fluke of a tail they've got. But that afternoon, I had seen the double fin easing through the water, maybe fifty feet out, sliding back and forth as easy as you please. It wasn't all that big a shark, maybe four foot or five, but big enough, I knew. So there I was, floating in the dark, remembering what I'd seen that afternoon and thinking about all the shark stories he'd ever told me. Not to mention that we weren't under the same shirt anymore. I called out for him; I didn't know what had happened. I wanted him to hold me, so I started paddling forward, trying to find him. But then I heard his voice shouting to stay still. That's when I felt it again, its side scraping my khaki pants like sandpaper. I was crying, I remember, with Daddy half whispering, "Hush, hush, they'll hear you." That really scared me. It hadn't occurred to me there might be more than one shark. "And don't take a crap," he warned, "they love the smell of shit."

So what happened?

Nothing. We didn't move for a minute or two—in the dark inside that shirt, all by myself, it felt like hours—and that was it. Gone. Daddy reached out and grabbed me, and got us organized again. Only this time I stayed under his shirt, hanging on his neck till he said I was going to choke him. That's when he told me the story.

You were just ten years old?

Worse things happen to kids. It did make me sad, though, the story. I didn't know who I felt worse for, the captain or his little girl. But that's how we got through the night. That and the singing.

Singing?

After all those hours in the water, the life jacket wasn't working so well. Like everything else in the boat, the vests were army surplus, so God knows how much use they'd seen already when we got them. I was floating lower and lower in the water; I had to tilt my head back after a while to keep it out of my mouth, the water. The cork had absorbed too much, I guess. I put my hands on my father's shoulders to keep from slipping deeper. Pretty soon, the life jacket was useless, but I kept it on as armor against the sharks. At least, that was what I was thinking as I hung on to my father. He was having a hard time staying awake, so he started singing. It was the only song I ever heard him sing.

What was that?

I don't know its name, but it goes like this:

If the ocean were whiskey,
and I were a duck,
I'd swim to the bottom
and never come up.

But the ocean's not whiskey,
and I'm not a duck,
so I'll play the jack of diamonds
and trust to my luck.

He just kept singing those same verses over and over again, like a chant more than a song. Then I started singing. It must have sounded strange out there in that dark marsh, those two voices carrying across the water. We kept at it a long time, waiting for the light.

The whole night in the water?

The whole night. Then, when the sun rose, we hauled ourselves up into the boat. There were a few straggling mosquitoes buzzing around us. I made a point of killing every one of them while Daddy tried the motor again. There was nothing doing, though, so Daddy tied a line to a bow cleat and, with water up to his chest, dragged the boat along the shelf of the mudflats for hours, it seemed, until he had hauled us to the mouth of the canal, where it joined the ship channel. He was so exhausted by the time we reached the edge of the flats he couldn't lift himself into the boat right away. He hung on by the gunnel, half floating for a few minutes until he had the strength to swing his leg over the side. I pulled him into the boat, and he lay on the deck like a fish. Lying there, he heard the trill of a motor off in the distance. Then, out in the channel, we saw a shrimper, its butterfly nets up and drying in the sun after a night of trawling. We got up on the benches and swung the life vests over our heads, shouting in the still air. I've never known another feeling like the one when the shrimp boat, still a hundred, two hundred yards out, swung its bow toward us.

And they towed you in?

Yeah. Daddy offered the skipper twenty dollars for his trouble and fuel. *"Oui, mon ami,"* he said—it was all still half French and half English back then—"but not for money." So he towed us in to Pointe à la Hache. We tied the boat up, walked down a shell road, and found a little diner that was just opening. Daddy called home, told Mama to come get us. Then we started eating, and when she got there an hour and a half later, we were still eating.

My God, what a night.

Well, it wasn't over yet. We still had to drive back to Delacroix, where we'd launched, to get our other car and the trailer. Then Mama and I drove home to New Orleans together while Daddy went back to Pointe à la Hache to get the boat. Every now and then she'd look at me and start crying. But it was strange. I wasn't hers anymore.

So that's how it happens? That's how they turn sweet little boys into big, mean men?

Something like that.

What was it he said? About the story, the story about the captain and his wife and daughter? You said that's what made you believe it.

When he got to the end of it, he said they had the photograph from the *Item*—the picture of those two columns of water, the one that ran in the paper—in some kind of archives on the third floor of the main library, down on Tulane Avenue.

Maybe that was part of the story he had heard?

No. What he said was all his own. He told me he had seen it once, the photograph, he and his father both. That's why I believed the story.

And that was all he said about it?

No, he said one other thing. Years later.

What was that?

He said they all end the same way, those sea stories. In madness or in death.

And what about this story?

It's not a story. It's true.

But how will it end?

End? With him singing, I guess, with the two of us singing—a man's deep, weary voice and a boy's thin little soprano, the voice of a drowned child, singing about whiskey and cards and a drunken duck—adrift in that black water, in that dark marsh, the mosquitoes hovering over our heads like death, and the two of us singing, singing until the sun comes up.